DYLAN'S HILL

DYLAN'S HILL

James Howerton

iUniverse LLC
Bloomington

DYLAN'S HILL

iUniverse books may be ordered through booksellers or by contacting:

iUniverse LLC
1663 Liberty Drive
Bloomington, IN 47403
www.iuniverse.com
1-800-Authors (1-800-288-4677)

ISBN: 978-1-4917-1871-1 (sc)
ISBN: 978-1-4917-1872-8 (hc)
ISBN: 978-1-4917-1873-5 (e)

Library of Congress Control Number: 2013923053

Printed in the United States of America.

iUniverse rev. date: 01/25/2014

ONE . . .

I figured that I had room for only two books in the overloaded F-100 pickup, and that was really depressing. I wonder if it was a mistake adapting the German Shepard puppy from the pound, as he took up some pretty valuable space, and seems more clueless than menacing. It's too late to think about that; the pup is entertaining, and some company. I'll probably need that.

If anyone out there will ever read this, I highly recommend the Reader's Digest BACK TO BASICS, and the HOUSEBUILDER'S BIBLE. Good luck finding them, but you never know. As I sit atop my adapted hill, in the wooded Abraham National Park where—before their mutual suicides— my parents had taken me camping, I feel stupidly lucky: I'd prepared for the big collapse over a year ago, spending all of the money from my parents' life insurance on MREs from Obie's Survival Store: water filters, two pairs of sturdy boots, and boxes and boxes of .22 rifle bullets. I'm lucky that I inherited almost everything else I needed; although the most important items were the heaviest. I already had a nylon dome tent and sleeping bag; I had my .22 semi-automatic rifle (20 round clip), all of the clothes I'd need; Levis jeans, cotton and flannel shirts, bales of socks and underwear. What weighed down the old Ford F-100 were the various knives, the hatchet and ax, two spades, two hammers, two 50-pound boxes of assorted nails, yards and yards of nylon rope, two pairs of pliers, one large one small—I went crazy; I know . . .

If anybody ever reads this, I'm Dylan. The six month old Shepard squatting beside me on the hill is Hans. He's scared.

I've been scared for a long time. Last names are probably not important anymore, especially for the dog. This is the place we camped when I was a kid, and there's still the old rusty iron grill here. The Madre Hills roll into the distance, and from up here you can see the old hiking trails wriggling grey through the forests of hickory, ash, oak, honey locust and cedar. Here is the overwhelming smell of trees. Below in the valley is the Kitawki River, where we caught blue gill and trout. I feel lucky here, and I've done the best I could. I've just turned 16, so it isn't like I'm mentally ready for this. But I got the old F-100 here, with a fiberglass shell for when it rains; I never thought I'd make it here alive. I did, and I create my mantra around this: I got that done, and I'm still alive. That's better than thinking about the other.

Back to my inventory, in case anyone ever reads this: eight cases of beef jerky from Olie's (he weighs 300 pounds and, even though he runs a survival store, I don't think he'll make it); 50 cans of Sterno, eleven boxes of stick matches, yards of fishing line (I already have my two rods and reels and full tackle boxes), a compass, two large bottles of penicillin, a box of anti-biotic creams, gauze bandages, disinfectant . . .

It's a peaceful day, for all that. I keep looking for something in the northern distance, smoke or something Apocalyptic, I don't know. Wind blows down the valley and rushes up this hill, bringing the smell of the river. Right now, sitting in this leafy evening, I know that I should get off my dead butt and get on with it. I know what I must do—before it gets dark—but I can't move just now. After that back in the city, I never thought I'd get my skinny life here, and I'm shaking with nerves. Hans whines at me and thumps his tail on the dirt. He can already sense when I'm a wimp.

"Better here than the pound, you punk," I tell him. My voice sounds spooky here in the quiet woods. I rub him as he snuggles up to me. He's afraid, and he's trusting me to take care of him. I hope he knows that one day I'll be trusting him to take care of me.

I keep my .22 on my lap and stare out over the wooded hills for signs of anything human. I suppose that'll be my life, at least for now. I feel lucky, and I think I might have stolen a march and got out just early enough. It'll probably take weeks yet.

Don't forget a solar-powered portable shower—I figured somehow it was worth the weight. Don't forget a solar battery light (LED). And a solar camp oven, the best you can get. I'm not going to make a fire until I have to. A large bow saw and a good lumber saw. Plastic tarp and tent pegs. A military camp spade. Two nylon backpacks, a good down coat. No guitar or harmonica, nothing that makes unnecessary noise . . .

I've thought this whole thing out—I think—but I'm no buff he-man. I sucked at football and baseball. How could we have been playing ball games, when it was all happening? It was stupid that I still wanted to be a rock star, even when I sensed—and then I knew—that it was happening. I know it's best to get my brain together, and another mantra comes to me: burn the past and worry about what is. I'm six foot tall, and not long ago girls had called me—cute. I guess that's good. I didn't have a girlfriend to escape with; it all came too soon and too late.

I hear the sound of something moving in the trees down the hillside—human or animal—I can't see anything. A deer? A black bear? I'm going to have to start paying attention to sounds out there.

Take nothing that requires gas. No chainsaw. Too much noise, and there won't be any gas. Forget batteries and anything that needs electricity, unless it's not heavy, and runs on solar batteries. I didn't take anything that would tell me what was going on; computers, Facebook, Media—because at the time I didn't want to know. That was a mistake.

Two steel plates, metal forks, spoons, tongs, skewer, iron cooking tripod and the best skillet you can find. Aluminum cook bowls, three Swiss army knives, twenty empty plastic water jugs and plastic funnel. Binoculars, two boxes of laundry soap, fishing net, vitamins, rubber tubing. I'd thought this out as best I could . . .

Why am I sitting here staring away rubbing on a stupid, whining puppy? You see it all coming, you Know it's coming, you try to get ready for when it comes, and now you know that you have to set up the campsite. It's already late evening; the sun falls into the west, in galactic colors. It's probably somewhere around May 17th, and that's lucky. I can always climb into the back of the F-100 and escape into sleep. I decide to do just that.

Before I finally rolled, I pumped myself full of carbohydrates and water; it's not that I feel tired up here over the river. Actually I'm feeling pretty wired, trying to get my brain around this; now that it finally Is.

No canned foods—they weigh too much. A tin camp coffeepot and 20 pounds of coffee. A gun oil kit and three cans of WD-40. Two big rolls of duct tape, three cases of Ramen noodles, a full needle-and-thread kit, light-weight aluminum fold-up camp chair and bed, a bale of paper towels, five boxes of large candles, twelve notebooks, one of which I'm writing in now. Ten boxes of pencils, a dozen packs of pens . . .

Hans, buddy, we're alone up here, and I'm scared. I keep going over my worldly goods; I'm having a hard time getting the inventory out of my brain after it's obsessed me for months. The forest around me rustles quiet. I think about what I was seeing in the city. Finally it's real.

I no longer hear the sound of whatever was down there. The wind is fresh and beautiful, and I pet Hans and try to stop the wahhhhing and remember what my mom and dad taught me when we came up here; about snakes, bears and cougars, about other people. Finally the night grows purple and I unload some supplies and climb with the pup into the back of the F-100, onto my soft sleeping bag. I hear an owl hoot, and the mad laughing of faraway coyotes. Hans grumbles at the strange primitive noises he can hear and I can't. He sounds like a little electric motor when he tries to be macho.

Damn it! I'm wired and I'm scared. I didn't think I'd make it alive to this place. You know now. Maybe you didn't know then, but you know now.

I'm sorry, but I wonder about all the people back in the city—what they're going through—and maybe someone I could have rescued—like in a story—and taken with me here, a girl. I could have somehow found more room, but I couldn't make more time. I love girls, but I'm not very good with girls. I keep thinking about them, the girls back in high school. It doesn't matter much now—but I can't help thinking about them.

I hear that rustling out there, something moving in the woods. I will learn to sleep with my arms around the .22 rifle, as if it were the girl I didn't bring.

Two . . .

Hans and me are up before sunset, and I get moving. I whisper my mantra, and it comforts me: Get this done; then get that done. What you have to do first is make a camp, and then make it disappear.

I set up the dome tent, driving the hard plastic pegs deep with the dumb side of the hatchet. It's a four-man tent, so we have enough room. Everything else stays in the camper, which I can padlock. Hans sniffs the area as if he's in heaven. He already has the confident legs of a Shepard, but he stays close to me. He's worthless as far as work goes. If he survives, he might turn out to be a very good partner. After living in a cage on a floor of concrete at the City Pound, it'll probably take some time for him to adjust to this, get his paleo—instincts back. Same with me, I suppose.

"Time for breakfast."

Hans thumps his tail and rubs on me. I'm still unnerved at the sound of my own voice. I open one of the MREs (beef stew) and spread its little solar panel to the morning sun. I forgot to mention powdered milk, which I have; but I'm more in the mood for coffee.

I carry two of the plastic jugs down the hillside to the river. I'd stumbled down this hillside since the age of five, three times each summer when we came here to camp. I know all of the trails and the best places to fish. I find the old flat boulder next to the current, squat down and fill the jugs. I'll use this familiar rock to clean fish on. I climb back up to my new home, Hans galloping excited in front of me. I start feeling confident now that I'm working and skills are coming back to me. I set up the solar oven and start the coffee. I feed Hans some puppy chow, give him a bowl of water, and as my MRE is cooking, I take up my binoculars and glass the entire area, particularly northwest, where about 13 miles away is the main highway. Most of the people won't try to escape into the wilderness, I reason. They'll stagger on past, looking for some civilization. There will be many people walking down that highway. They will believe a highway leads somewhere.

A chilly May morning, and the woods are alive with bird songs. When my beef stew is done, I sit back on the camp chair and wolf it down with a bitter cup of hot coffee. Beef stew for breakfast? It sounded good, and it is. Well, I've got all of my supplies inventoried and put away. I got the truck in here, but it will never leave this place. I'll camouflage it with cedar limbs. I find myself gazing up at the sky; but I doubt there will be very many planes flying anymore.

I wash out my tin coffee cup, brush my teeth, get moving. With the ax I chop cedar branches in a mess of trees 50 yards or so in the woods and haul them to the campsite. Cedars are abundant, and they stay green awhile. An hour later the tent is just a big lump of green. I take a break and sit staring out at the river valley, at crows and hawks sailing the wind. I pluck two ticks off of Hans. Already I feel a terrible stab of loneliness; I should have brought a human companion with me, a human to talk to. It happened too fast for perfect planning.

Do this until it's done; then do that. This is the first day of a lot of days. I'm going to have to just make a good camp and then wait.

It's important that I make everything invisible. I even drive the pickup, on its final drinks of gas, up to the top of the trail, hook a nylon rope to a big dead tree, and haul it across the way. At least nobody else will be driving in here. It feels good to work, use my muscles, concentrate on the job at hand and not think about anything else. I chop more cedar branches, haul them down and camo the F-100. A good truck and a good friend that will never leave this final resting place. It's about 2 o'clock, I figure, when I've got all this done. My body gives me a sudden hint, and I know what my next job is.

Slinging the .22 over my shoulder, I hike about 100 yards away and find a fallen log where I can drop trou and sit. I use the camp spade to dig out a deep and wide latrine. No sink, no bathtub, no shower. I only have about 50 rolls of toilet paper; but if I live far enough into the future, there are always plenty of leaves. At this point, it's stupid to think about the future, even though I think I've planned for it.

I return to my camp and look it over. Other than being a small clearing in the woods on a hill over the river, it looks uninhabited. I'll have to remember to religiously put everything away, at least until I know what's going on out there. Hans can't get enough of this new Eden; he comes galloping up with a big grin on his face. He's my only friend now, and he doesn't know squat about rattlesnakes.

When I'm sure everything is hidden, I relax on the camp chair and consider taking my fishing gear down to the river to try my luck. The MREs will last forever if I don't eat them up; but sooner or later I'm going to have to start supplementing the diet with fish and game. I'm too lazy right now, so I celebrate my first day by heating up another MRE (fish and chips), and reheating the coffee. I share the pub treat with Hans. The game I don't really want right now; the rabbits might have ring-worm, and the squirrels will have fleas.

A few more things I took when I escaped: dozens of packets of ketchup, mustard and other condiments in the little restaurant bags. Not environmentally sound, I guess; but who's going to care about that anymore? The knives you want: a big buck knife, a good filet knife, a set of steak knives, a skinning knife. No butter knives; you can spread things out with a spoon. Ten blocks of paraffin wax, a light plastic rain coat and pants, a fifty pound bag of cornmeal. A pocket mirror, vegetable seeds for growing a garden, trail mix, salt, sunflower seeds, 40 bars of soap, five terrycloth towels, a wire brush . . .

I keep staring at the sky. It doesn't look like it's going to rain, but it will one day. I spend the rest of this day cutting water channels around my tent, lining them with stones. This is the rainy season, and I don't want to get washed down into the river. Finally it grows dark, and I congratulate myself for what I've accomplished on my first full day here. I'm sore and tired, and I want to stay that way for now. I sit on the camp chair, sip my coffee, rub Hans on the back and stare at the sunset. Maybe I should have brought something from my other world: my I-pad or laptop. But those days are over, and I don't want to face the day when batteries run out. I don't want to hear anything that might be on the radio or the internet right now. Those days are over.

Three sharpening stones, a straightedge razor if you can find one (mine belonged to my great-grandfather), dog food until it runs out, two pairs of scissors. I wanted to buy a shotgun, but by that time there were no more shotgun shells to be had. I probably couldn't hit the sky with a pistol, but I'm pretty good with the .22 rifle . . .

Hans whines at the moon, a full, silent pumpkin peeking over the eastern hills.

"Just you and me now, Pal. It's better than the dog pound. And tonight we sleep in the tent."

I stare northwestward, wondering if I would be able to see headlights on the highway. Surely I wasn't the only one to get out, a scared teenager, still a virgin. I don't see anything but the dark forest. I try and avoid thinking about my folks and why they did what they did; wondering why this all happened to me . . . feeling sorry for myself. I'm afraid it happened to everybody. Hans feels nervous in the quiet, although he already adores this place in the trees, and the wind smell swooping over the river and up the hillside. If he encounters a rattlesnake, he'll probably want to make friends and play with it. He's afraid, like I am, but not about the wildlife.

I figure it's got to come down to just honing in on one thing that needs to be done; and when it's done, honing in on something else. I can recharge myself sitting here on the camp chair taking in the beautiful river valley; I can keep strong working and eating. If I don't get stupid, if I ration right now in the beginning, I can last a long time on this hill. At least until I know what's out there; if there is anything out there. I'm sure there is. There are better Doomsday Preppers than me out there; some of them wouldn't even have had to leave their homes. It's only been a few days; it hasn't hit the fan yet.

It will. I'm not some paranoid nine-eleven, in case you're thinking that. I can't say what happened back there, how long it's going to take, or what's going to happen next. It's only one day here on this hill. I'll make it my fox den and go on from there. I'll make it My fox den.

"I name this Dylan's Hill," I say to Hans, who sits Shepard-alert staring at the great orange moon.

THREE . . .

Before sunrise, Hans and I climb down to the river and I manage to catch 3 good-size bluegills.

I skin and gut them with my filet knife on the flat stone, and chuck the guts into the river. I carry the filets up to my camp and open the solar grill. I roll the fish filets in cornmeal and fold them in aluminum foil (I forgot to mention aluminum foil. I have ten rolls of it).

Exhausted from his first fishing trip, Hans curls up and snores as the fish bake in the solar oven. It's close to noon by the sun (yes, I thought about bringing a self-wind wristwatch, but they weren't to be found, and what good is it to know the exact time of day?). I don't like the dark clouds that are forming in the west, over the tall hills that rise above the river. A chilly wind is flowing from the west, and it already smells like rain. I make sure everything has been put away . . . but studying my camp, I get a strange feeling that something isn't quite right.

When the fish are done, I eat them with some powdered potatoes. The potatoes taste really bad, but I'm sadly lacking in vegetables, and the vitamins won't last forever. I clean up camp and inspect my water channels. They should funnel rainwater around the camp and down the hillside. I hear thunder in the distance. The clouds are gathering and moving this way like black pillows. The wind is picking up, smelling storm-fresh. By the time I relieve myself at the latrine, the wind is gusting, and a light mist tickles my face. I sit in the camp chair and watch the storm move in.

But I keep feeling something strange. I look back and study my campsite. Hans, sniffing around the hidden pickup truck, looks up at me and cocks his head. Nothing looks disturbed—I think. I get out my binoculars and sweep the area. The looming storm sends prickles down my neck. I go up and study the truck. One of the camper windows . . . the dust has been swept away. Did I do that?

When the rain sweeps in, I crawl with Hans into the cedar-smothered tent, taking the fold-up chair with me. Hans sits alert and fearful, and he jumps and whines when a lightning bolt strikes, sending a roar up the river. There's nothing to do but sit and wait it out. No television, no laptop, no music. The rain patters down; then hammers the hill. The storm is going to blow away the cedar limbs and ruin my camouflages. But I still want to keep this place invisible—that seems very important, at least for now. I sit in the tent and listen to the rain and wind. There would be bad storms and really bad storms; in a few months there would be cold and snow. I keep the panic down by concentrating on the jobs ahead of me when it dries up out there. The first must be to replace any cedar limbs that might blow off the tent and truck. I try not to think that, when I was fishing down on the river, something was in my camp.

There aren't that many dangerous animals out here: snakes, black bears, and a rare cougar or two. I worry more for Hans than myself. He's curled up on the sleeping bag, listening to the storm, and giving me a scared look. His short life, before this 'adventure', was spent in kennels and cages. For him, this is probably like Dorothy stepping out of the farmhouse and into Oz.

When the storm dies off, I crawl out and check on the damage; there's almost none, and that gives me a pat-on-the-back of confidence: not much camo got blown off. This is a relatively level campsite, used by people for so long that the clay has been stamped into a hard table that sheds rain. I should have brought a plastic welcome mat; Hans is going to stomp his muddy paws into the tent. What a stupid thing to even worry about.

I arrange the camos on the tent and truck, making again two lumps of green. Anyone who might have come into this camp would be able to figure it out. From any distance, it is—I hope—invisible. I sit on the camp chair and watch the storm move off to the east.

I keep going from should I avoid people, or look for them? For now I think it's best to avoid, although I'm already hungry for news of how it went down there, how it's going. I suppose I feel that I belong here as much as the city; I never felt I belonged there. I didn't have friends to speak of, and it never really bothered me being alone. This is something beyond that, of course. I miss a few people from the old life; I miss my parents. But what good is it to dwell on the past? It's only now to do the Robinson Crusoe, keep busy and stay on the lookout. I hope this doesn't seem cold. I'm only 16, and I know I'm not even close to the true Doomsday Preppers. We all believed it would happen—and we all believed that it would never happen. Now it's happened, and I feel like I'm living in a dream.

I feed Hans his puppy chow, and prepare myself a lunch of beef jerky and trail mix. I won't try my solar shower out until tomorrow, maybe, if the sun's shining. Another big item I forgot to mention: I packed twelve boxes of alcohol wipes.

I get out my plastic gallon jugs, climb down to the river, and fill them. The Kitawki River flows over granite and sand, so its water is pretty clean. I have sterilizing tablets and water filtration devices. This river water is good enough to wash with unfiltered. I make four trips, hauling the water jugs up and hiding them in cedar limbs. A sweet cedar smell is beginning to linger in the camp. I think about how I can make some sort of thing to catch rainwater and funnel it into the jugs. Today, that would have saved me a lot of work.

The sun is still behind overcast, so I have to eat a cold dinner. I suppose I should have packed some canned fruits and vegetables. I sit and munch trail mix and jerky. The sky is calm, and I can see the smeary light of the moon behind the clouds. Far to the north the horizon is unusually dark, and I wonder if another storm is out there. But then I see a distant line of red below the sky, and I know that what is out there is not a storm but a great fire.

I stare through my binoculars and think, 'Good God! What does that mean?'

The city is sixty miles away; but maybe there are fires everywhere. I wonder what I'll do if a fire reaches here. That would pretty much seal my doom. I spent months thinking this out, writing things down, making notes on my computer, trying to get myself in shape, in mountain man mode.

I never thought once about a forest fire.

FOUR . . .

Day Three. Smoke hangs over the northern horizon, but the wind is strong out of the south, thank God. I can't see the red line of flames, but the smoke puts a bit of a knot in my stomach. I decide to begin each morning glassing the area. The binoculars reveal nothing but trees blowing in the wind. I eat a piece of jerky, feed and water Hans, and put away my camp chair.

"Let's go fishing, Good Pup."

I catch a nice bass, which is more than enough for lunch. I filet it and climb back up the hill, as quietly as I can; I suppose it's good to stay paranoid for a while. I set up the camp stove and get the bass baking. Hans has wandered into the woods east of camp, and I go after him. The dork doesn't know what might be out there. I find him sniffing at something under a big oak tree, and I wish I had a shotgun for snakes. I'll have to cut an ash branch and make a snake-stick.

"What are you sniffing at, Hans?"

I kneel down and my spine shudders: I stare at the boot prints. They have to be fresh. I glance around the woods, but there's no sign of anything human. There are no prints at my campsite, so maybe whoever made them is as wary as I am. I resist the urge to call out; I'm carrying a rifle, but maybe he is too. I put my boot against the prints and judge them to be a size 6 or 7. At least it's not Goliath.

Again I study the woods. The intruder hadn't come into my camp, maybe because after the rain I'd spot his boot prints immediately. The woods are misty this day, the trees moving lazy in the wind, forest birds singing but not alarmed. I know that it's good to have blue jays and crows around you, if you want a good alarm system. The smell of the baking bass breaks me out of my shock.

I eat lunch and drink plenty of water. The filtered water is tasteless, but I know I need to stay hydrated. Some people planning for this sort of thing would bring bottled water, but it's too heavy, and soon enough you'll run out. Find top quality tablets and filters that will make the water you find safe. It's the most important thing you can do.

I keep staring around the woods, thinking about those boot prints. Maybe they're old; I've only been here three days. No, I think they're very new; that means somebody knows I'm here, and somebody doesn't want to make himself known. I'd better keep the rifle close and stay in camp for now; I'm already sick of fish anyway.

The smoke in the far north has dissipated, and that's a relief. But I'm still worried about wandering too far from camp. Sooner or later I'm going to have to. I keep thinking about those boot prints.

"Better make it later," I say to Hans, who's sleeping in the shade.

I sit on the camp chair and listen; there's no sound but the river, the birds and the wind. Does the guy have a campsite nearby? Is he alone? Does he have a high-powered rifle that makes my .22 laughable? He might be a survivalist who jumped the gun as I did; it wouldn't be anybody from the city, unless he drove here. What might or might not come from the city would probably not be for a few days—or maybe weeks. I've heard no car or truck drive up the trail. When I was a kid, Dad had a killer jeep, and we would easily go off road and bounce up the trail to this place. The F-100 barely made it here, stumbling and cracking apart on its last run.

I would hear a motorcycle or a 4-wheeler. I think about going back and studying the boot prints again, but what good would that do? It's not like I'm Daniel Boone.

I spend the rest of the afternoon spreading grass over the water channels, cutting and shaping a good snake-stick, tidying up camp and digging a trash hole. The sun is beating down, so I set up the portable shower, carefully spreading open its solar panels, and fill it with water. I'll have to go down and get more water for clothes and cooking; but I decide to do it tomorrow. If I want to be anywhere near human I'll have to find a way to catch rainwater.

While my shower water is heating up, I break out an MRE for dinner (spaghetti and meat sauce). Hans wakes up hungry, and I give him some puppy chow. As the sun falls slowly into the hills I take a shower and put on clean clothes. I sit on the camp chair and eat dinner, and it's very satisfying. When I'm out camping, I seem to be hungry all the time, and practically everything tastes good. It feels good to be clean and wearing clean clothes.

It's getting dark when I put everything away and bury my trash. The thought occurs to me to one day fashion some makeshift table; that will keep me busy for a day. I watch the stars come out and idly point out the constellations to Hans, who sits peacefully at my side. The woods are misty in the dark, as if whispering gossamer. I'm about to doze off when Hans startles me with a growl, then a sharp bark. I clutch my rifle and stare into the misty woods. Suddenly, the hackles rise on Hans' back, and he gallops into the dark.

"Hans, you idiot! get back here," I hiss at him. *"Hans!"*

Growling, then silence. Then a voice—a girl's soft voice: "You're just a big puppy. You're a good dog, Hans. I'd put that rifle down if I were you."

The girl creeps out of the dark. She's holding a pistol on me, and I put down my rifle.

"Don't . . . I'm friendly!" I say in astonishment. "I'm friendly. Please don't shoot."

She stands in the faint moonlight and studies me. She wears blue jeans and a flannel shirt and boots. She couldn't be more than a hundred pounds, but she might as well be a serial killer with that pistol aimed at me. She has long brown hair in a braid; she's wearing a baseball cap, so I can't really make out her face.

"You're friendly," she says, with some amusement. "That's a strange name. Glad to meet you, Friendly."

"Yeah . . . hey, would you mind not pointing that thing at me?"

"I could have shot you two days ago if I'd wanted to."

"That's—well, that's good. You . . . startled me coming out of the dark. Are you . . . like camping up here?"

"Yes, I'm like camping up here—like you."

Jeez, she's snotty. "Are you alone?" I ask her.

"Maybe." She's studying me. I have the paranoid thought that she's been watching me for a while, and probably saw me get out of my shower, jay-bird naked. "You don't look very old," she says.

"You don't either. Are you—hungry or anything? I have trail mix, beef jerky, a few chocolate bars."

She walks into the campsite and abruptly sits down cross-legged on the ground, her pistol at ready. I can see her face now, and she's pretty. To be honest, pretty girls have always scared me; and I have a feeling that any sudden move could get my head blown off.

"How old are you?" she demands.

"I'm sixteen." At least I'm not a liar.

"God, sixteen." She frowns at the woods. "I know you're by yourself here. I thought you were older than 16." She waves the pistol around in disgust. "This is a mistake. You're a friggin kid."

I can't believe my ears. "You're not very friendly," I tell her. "What are you doing up here?"

"Yes, I'd like a chocolate bar. And something to drink. Please."

I get up and—slowly—get my snack bag out of the tent. "All I've got is filtered water. It tastes flat, but it's safe. So, what brings you up here?"

"What brings you up here? You're packed like you want to build a cabin or something."

"Maybe I will someday. What brings me up here—I think you know the answer to that." I give her two chocolate bars and the bottle of water. "Are you alone?"

"So far." She puts the pistol in her lap in order to unwrap the chocolate bars. She's very pretty; and she's built like an athlete. But I told you before that I'm not good at talking to girls. She sits munching the chocolate, watching me under her ball cap as if I were a dork—which I probably am.

"I didn't expect to see anybody up here." I try out a smile; she's absently petting Hans, and she probably figures by now that I'm not dangerous. "What brings you up here?"

"The rocks."

"The rocks?"

"I'm a rock climber—was a rock climber. I've been up here a week."

"I wish I'd left a month ago," I say. "I barely made it out."

"Pretty bad, eh?"

"Yeah, it was. Really fast and really bad."

Her face crinkles a little, but she doesn't seem to be a girl who outright cries. Maybe she's as lonely as I am by now, but she sure doesn't show it.

"I've got plenty of supplies," I say, looking away from her face. "I'm pretty well prepared."

"I saw that. You're good at fishing."

"Thanks." I try to imagine how dorky I seem. I look at the ground. "I'm sure you came up here knowing about—that. What was happening . . ."

"I don't want to talk about it. I don't want to think about it."

"You saw the fire north of here."

"I don't want to talk about it!"

"Okay!"

I let an uncomfortable silence fall. "I'm Dylan," I finally say. "Friendly's just a nickname."

I get a very short laugh out of her; then the silence falls again. After about half a minute, she suddenly gets to her feet. "Well, gotta go. So long, Dylan."

"Uh . . . you're going . . ."

"I have a flashlight." She turns and marches into the darkness of the forest, leaving me staring.

"Hey, wait!" I call to her. "What's your name?"

Her face appears from the trees and she puts an urgent index finger to her lips. "Shhhh! Don't be making noise like that. Don't yell or call out—you shouldn't even talk out loud."

"Why? No, please don't go—why?"

"You'd better know why. My name's Julie." She stares out of the shadows. "I'll be around."

FIVE . . .

No, I don't sleep this night. I keep thinking about her as if she wasn't real, as if that whole thing . . . but I haven't been up here long enough to hallucinate, not like that. I have the tent flap open, and I bend my ear to any sound that might come from out there. Surely I'd hear people out there—but I hadn't heard Julie. It's strange thinking her name, and remembering her coming out of the dark, like a lynx.

She wasn't up here to rock climb. There are probably more than her out there; maybe a lot more. Sooner or later they'll get hungry. I push that thought away: you can't waste your brain inventing bad things that can happen. I packed my gear; I planned and prepared; I staked this hill, and it's Dylan's Hill.

Julie. Was she good or really bad? Only, I didn't want her to leave. At least I know that I'm not the last person out here. I tell myself that tomorrow I'll get the guts to go out and explore a little. But I've never seen anything through the binoculars. Three days without any sign of humans, until Her. I'll go snoop a little anyway, at least up to the nearest hiking trail. The tallest nearby hill would be a good place to really sweep the valley with glasses; but it's a good half day's hike from here. I haven't seen any lights, I haven't seen any campfire smoke; I haven't heard anything.

Hans snores on the sleeping bag, next to my leg. I start to get very ridiculous ideas about Julie—and yeah, I know—we had a real short and bizarre conversation while she was holding a gun on me, and she got up and left a little rudely. I wonder what kind of gear and supplies she has. Two can survive better than one. She left here in the dark; she can't be camped that far away. Why hadn't I detected her? She said she was alone—for now. What did that mean?

What happened was, she heard the F-100 drive in here; it had sounded like a dying elephant, and she'd been spying on me from day one. I smile, but it's kind of a crooked one. I wonder how prepared she is—and had she seen it coming as I did? She moves as if she's been jogging and working out forever. Probably a cheerleader in those lost times, with that face and body. I obviously hadn't made much of an impression on her. She complimented my fishing. How's that for cool.

It's comforting knowing she's here. And that she said she'd be around. The dark tent doesn't seem as smothering as it has been. I can't imagine how loud Hans is going to snore when he's full grown. I listen for sounds out there in the dark woods. She can't be camped too far away. Maybe she feels I've invaded her stakeout or something—though it is—used to be—a public forest. I want to talk to her about when she thinks people from the city are going to pour into this place—maybe none. I want to ask her if she thinks anything else is going to come from the city. She wouldn't want to talk about that. If she's been stalking me for three days, why does she seem so damn unfriendly? I want to ask her how long, she thinks, it's going to take.

Hans likes her. Julie.

Six . . .

She's still in my brain, of course, when I crawl out and look at the dawn. I immediately glass the woods all round, seeing only the woods. Hans plods out of the tent and yawns widely. She disappeared into the woods at night; that's more than I would do. Why hadn't I ever seen her flashlight?

I GRE a breakfast of eggs, bacon, hash browns and toast. I make up a jug of instant milk. Hans and I have our breakfast in the chilly wind. I spend 15 minutes cleaning camp; then I go back to the camp chair. What will I say to her when I see her again? Ask questions, see if she knows anything about what's going on out there.

I sit like a rag doll and think about her until Hans whines and nips at my hand.

"Ow, you little dick! Yeah yeah yeah." I drag my butt out of the chair and we (I!) make several heavy trips up from the river with water. I camo the jugs. I have a water supply. I glass the woods again. The smoke is gone from the northern horizon, and it looks to be a glorious day when it warms up. What day is it, May 21st? It might be important to keep track of the date, but I probably won't. I make as little noise as possible, but it's not like I'm bothering anybody. I remind myself that this is Dylan's Hill, by way of conquest. I wasn't the one to scare Her to death slinking out of the dark with a pistol in my hand.

You sit out here all alone, and suddenly a pretty girl appears out of the woods . . . . oh wait, she's aiming a gun at you.

I wander into the woods and make my way up to the hiker trail. I don't know what I expect, but it's nothing. Only the woodland quiet. Wherever she's camping, she's not making campfires. If anybody else is out there, none of them are making campfires. Not yet. I haven't seen any battery lights, but I'm sure there are a lot of them out there.

I head back a different route to the camp. Maybe she took advantage of my long absence, and ripped off my tent. Halfway back down I spy a coyote sitting in the trees, staring at me and Hans. The coyote is like a statue, and Hans doesn't even know he's there. I'm sure he's not the only one. I wonder if they sense how fast the world out there is collapsing. That's too much for me.

I get into camp and take a quick inventory. No sign of rock-girl. Hans flops down, exhausted, and is asleep in minutes. I start some coffee and slouch down in the camp cot. I should be dead-dog tired, but my body buzzes and I can't get her out of my mind. Maybe she'll pay another visit tonight; maybe she's a night stalker. Maybe I'll never see her again; she didn't seem to like me much. I didn't lie about my age; I didn't lie about anything. I didn't even brag.

Maybe I should have bragged. She's probably used to guys who brag a lot. Who are they now? What are they now? I gaze out over the river at the peaceful hills. It's probably three o'clock or so. My dinner is mixed nuts and sunflower seeds. I sip coffee and—

She walks out of the woods and into my campsite. Seeing her in full daylight, I'm stupefied. Her face is a little smudged, and she's obviously been hiking the woods. She's wearing the same baseball cap, and I notice it's a Cubs hat. She is very pretty, but also a bit grubby. Again she Indian-squats on the ground and looks at me.

"You're not aiming a pistol at me," I say to her, after a few moments.

"No, not this time. Can you use that rifle?"

"Yes."

"Good. Semi-automatic with a big clip?" she asks.

"20 rounds."

"Good." She nods thoughtfully at the woods. Hans has come awake and has his traitorous head in her lap. She rubs him as if she'd adapted him. "I want to borrow something from you."

I give her a suspicious look. "What?"

"Your portable shower." She frowns at the woods. "And some of your bath soap."

"Okay. You can use it here—"

"No."

"Look, I'm not some pervert. You want to take a shower, I'll go fishing."

"No." She gets up suddenly, like a gymnast springing from the floor, and Hans jumps back. "Okay, just thought I'd ask. Goodbye."

"No, wait!" I get up from the chair. "Sure you can borrow it, and some soap. Jeez, I was just trying to save you from—"

"Nobody says 'jeez' anymore. And you can't save me from anything."

"Take the damn shower!" I glare down at the river. Then I glare at her. "Go on, take it. You need to wash your clothes, that's for sure; so I'll throw in some laundry detergent."

She laughs. "Laundry detergent."

"Yeah." I study her; she has a very elfin, cheerleader face and body. Every prancing pretty, stuck-up girl who never looked at me in high school. "How old are you?" I ask.

"I'm eighteen." She looks at me like that's a great age chasm. Maybe it is.

"Look . . . Julie: if we got together—I mean, our supplies and that—we'd stand a better chance if we're together." I can't believe I say that. It's not Shakespeare.

Her face darkens. "I don't think it's a good time in human history to play well together."

"What makes you say that?"

"Look, Dylan . . ."

"Okay, take the shower and soap. I'm going to need it back in a couple of days."

"Thank you."

She carries the solar shower into the woods and I sit back down, wondering if I'll ever see it again. Okay, I was a good neighbor. And she's got serious Rude-problems. I stare into the woods. Just like that she shows up, and just like that she's gone. What is her problem?

I guess that's a no-brainer. Everybody out there must be crazy now, even me. I don't think 'problems' quite describes it. She hasn't got soap, so maybe one day she'll return. I chew on a handful of trail mix and scratch Hans on the back. The trek up to the trail and back has my legs aching. I don't feel like moving. I sip coffee and watch the sun go down.

At sunset she ghosts into the camp with my solar shower. She's washed and is wearing a clean pair of jeans and a red Nebraska tee shirt. No ball cap. Her hair falls auburn down her shoulders. She knows how to shock a guy, I'll give her that.

"Are—are you hungry?" I ask, jumping out of my camp chair. "Here, sit down; I'll take the ground this time."

She sits down in the camp chair, drying her hair in the wind, and sighs at the growing gloom. "Damn, I miss electricity. I miss electricity."

"Yeah." I sit down on the ground and pet Hans. "The sun's going down, or I could fix a hot meal. But I have trail mix, jerky, all sorts of good stuff."

"Do you have toothpaste?" She gives me a look.

"Yes. I have a lot of toothpaste."

"I'm almost out. I came in here on foot. When I heard your truck, I couldn't believe somebody could get it in here."

"I know this place," I say. "I've camped here all my life."

"All sixteen years." She gives me a smile—I don't know if it's sweet or sour.

"It's not like you're some adult," I say to her.

"No, it isn't." She chews on a handful of trail mix; I give her a bottle of drinking water. I wish I could cook a gourmet meal from my GRE stash; but you need the sun, and it's already dark. She's a presence that's beyond me, and I don't want her to just stand up and leave again. The forest is in dark mist; somewhere out there I hear my owl.

"You want to watch a movie?" she asks.

"A what?"

"A movie. I have a solar battery Tablet with a lot of movies loaded. Music too, but we can't listen to music, and there can't be any sound on the movie."

". . . okay . . ."

Julie sets up the small screen in her lap and loads the movie. Terminator VI. If you've ever seen Terminator VI without the sound, you know it's pretty confusing. But it feels great leaning close to her to watch the screen. She smells very fresh with the wind blowing through her hair. I wish I had popcorn or something. Being this close to her, I can't get the lump out of my throat.

When the movie's over, it's black under a misty moon. Julie turns off the Tablet. We sit in the quiet darkness.

"That was my first movie date," I say. Instinctively we keep our voices down.

She smiles in the faint moonlight. "And it was a silent one."

"Uh . . . Julie . . . it's pretty dark. You can stay here tonight; Hans and I can sleep in the camper, and you can have the tent."

"Thanks . . . but no. I have to go."

Just like that she vanishes into the darkness. I pet Hans and I can't hold back a smile. That wasn't such a bad first date—considering the circumstances. She's way Cheerleader out of my league, but maybe there aren't a lot of leagues anymore. Before I crawl into the cedars to sleep, I stare into the dark and see her flashlight bounce through the woods, going north. Okay, she lives north of me.

I chuckle and rub Hans. "I'm already sharing a shower with her."

SEVEN . . .

Day four I hear a jeep or truck.

I'm sitting in camp with the Back to Basics manual nearby, trying to make a camp chair. I've chopped ash branches for the frame and shaved them with my pocket knife. I'm now cutting rope and studying knots. With acres of wood everywhere and plenty of tools, you'd be surprised how hard it is to make a simple chair. I want to impress Julie, I guess.

That doesn't matter now. I listen to the sound of the vehicle to try and determine how far away it is. I have to squeeze Hans quiet. I hear the jeep (or whatever it is), gun its engine and struggle. It's not on the trail I drove the truck in. It's northeast . . . a mile away?

I sit and listen to the gunning engine. Is the guy stuck? No, the vehicle rackets up the northeast hill, and in twenty minutes is just a distant roar. I sit and rub Hans. Maybe it's beginning. But I have no idea what could be beginning.

Get this done—and then get that done. I have to keep my mind that simple, and not get crazy-jumpy over a jeep driving into a national park. I wonder where Julie is, if she heard it. They went northeast, and I can no longer hear them. Are they that far away, or have they parked it? They're probably friendly and scared and hopefully not too freaked out. I think I know the trail they took; it climbs the northeast hill; then meanders down to Echo Lake. We fished there a few times, and you really did hear echoes there. It's like a natural amphitheater. I convince myself that that's where they went. Fresh water, campsites everywhere.

I wonder where Julie is. They're people, just like you, I tell myself. You're going to have to get the scared out. Pussies get scared. You're more scared than Julie. You knew they'd come, those who know the preserve. I get back to my chair, that's job one. I'll need it for when Julie comes to visit—in her own strange way. And building caveman furniture keeps your mind focused.

I wonder where she is.

Three hours later I have what you can sit on, at least. It looks more like bad folk art than a usable chair that's going to hold up. It's about 4 o'clock by the sun. I feed Hans and then stretch my legs to the latrine. I haven't heard anything—the jeep or other sounds. Echo Lake is . . . what, maybe three miles away? That's where they went; maybe a lot of them will escape there. I wonder what they think of all this. I don't think anybody's going to be driving up my trail to my hill. I could be very, very wrong.

I open an MRE (beef stroganoff), thinking the aroma might get Julie's attention. I open the solar oven and start some coffee. If you can make coffee, there's a false sense of having everything you need. I constantly watch the woods, like some freaked-out paranoid. I should Want to get together with the folks who flee here; but like Julie, I'm too scared to trust anybody. That might be later, but it's not now. Most of the folks in the city are waiting for it to be fixed, to come back on again. What if it doesn't?

I sit on my ash chair and eat the stroganoff. There's even a thick slice of garlic bread to munch on. I give a chunk of it to Hans.

"What are we going to do when the dog food runs out, Hansy? What are we going to do when the military food runs out?"

"You'll be where I am," a soft voice from the trees. Julie comes into camp and studies me in my comical home-made chair. She sits down in the aluminum camp chair and pets Hans. "They drove off down to Echo Lake." She gives me a look.

"I thought so. It's a national park, people drive in and—"

"Don't start that with me, Dylan. You're a sixteen year old boy out here. And I think you know how it's going to get, when they realize nothing's going to come back on. You've been an obsessed Doomsday Prepper for how long? Well, here it is."

I stare at her mad face: "You're an eighteen year old girl. And you're more stuck-up than . . ." I swat at something that might be stuck-up. I look at her. "Are you hungry?"

She looks back. "Yes."

"Okay, name your meal, and I'll bet I can cook it."

"Can I have some coffee?"

"Of course. You don't have to ask." I fetch another cup (take very lightweight plastic ones), and pour her a coffee.

She sips the coffee. "Stuck-up. That's . . . they don't say that anymore, Dylan."

"I know. That's why I do. Now, the game is Name your Meal and Stump the Cook. Come on."

She laughs. It's a beautiful laugh and I know that, in spite of everything rational, I'm falling in love with her. She's not in love with me, of course. She's here because she's hungry, and I have food. Is that what it's all going to come down to? Me destroying myself for a stuck-up . . .

"Swedish meatballs," she says.

"Come on; that's too easy. But, Swedish meatballs it is." I rummage through the MREs and find it. I set it in the sun and spread out its magic wings. "Anything to munch on while you wait?" I ask.

"Maybe some trail mix, please."

While she's crunching down trail mix, I rummage in my supplies and find it, the great plastic bag of memories. I vowed to save them. I vowed to not break this open until I needed memories; it's my holy bag of memories, of good times and years gone past.

But, what the hell. I tear open the plastic bag and cherry scents the air. I take it over and wave it in front of her. "I should save this for dessert. The greatest candy in history."

She reads the bag. "Twizzlers."

"Cherry Twizzlers. Greatest candy ever—and I'm not a candy fan."

"Yeah. You don't have a Snickers, do you?"

"No, they melt."

"So does licorice."

I take the first luscious cherry rope out of the bag and nibble at it. I know I'm acting like a fool, but you shouldn't just chew a cherry Twizzler, you should nibble; then chew the niblets. "Try one."

She's a nibbler too. She's hungry, that's the only reason she's here. She doesn't care anything about me, and I'm not going to be some puppy dog around her.

"It's not bad," she says as she chews. "Not a Snickers bar, but it's got sugar for energy."

I refill her coffee cup and she steals four Twizzlers from the bag.

"Snickers has to be a close second," I remark.

"No. You get a lot more from a Snickers bar than a little rope of licorice. They're probably not making either one of them anymore, so why does it matter?"

"Okay, you don't like the dessert. Let's try the main course."

She sits on the camp chair and gobbles down the MRE. She likes to talk with her mouth full: "You haven't called me a bitch yet."

"No . . . was I supposed to?"

She's full, and she lets Hans lick away the last of the meal. "I miss electricity. I keep thinking of t.v. That's pretty sad, isn't it?"

I'm looking at her, wondering how her face could be so soft and so hard at the same time. "I guess it's pretty and sad."

"A sixteen year old philosopher." She sighs. "Maybe it'll all come back again."

"Maybe. They might have prepared, the government or somebody. Surely somebody out there can do something."

"The nights are so black," she says. "When I came out here I thought, 'Oh, it'll only be a week or two, like before', even though I knew better. I'd wait here for the glow to come back. It hasn't come back yet, and maybe it never will. Even if it doesn't come back, I'm going back."

"Back to the city? For a guy."

"Yes, a guy." She's staring across the river valley with tragic eyes. Her eyes are I guess what you call hazel.

I feel like crap all the sudden. Like a fool. "Your boyfriend."

"Yes, my boyfriend. Let's drop the subject. Just so you know; one morning I'll be gone."

"Okay." We sit in the dark woods. I know what she means about the night sky being too black. This is a blackness we've never seen in our lives. I wonder what happened to the glow and the reflection off clouds, of the city. Why wouldn't she have a boyfriend? Why didn't he come here with her? No, I'm not going to ask.

"I'm really starting to miss a lot of things," she says. "It's one thing to camp here and another to think about living here. I can't imagine just—this."

"You said you weren't going to think about it."

"How can you not?" She gives Hans a hug. I wonder if I'll ever get one. "But you're right."

"I mean, we don't really know anything yet. We should just stay here and wait and see. Do some fishing or something."

"We? God, I'm crazy." She smiles at me. I'm in shock when she gets up, walks over and kisses me on the lips. "Are you up for a hike?"

"A hike . . . yeah." She kissed me. "A hike where?"

"Come on, Mountain Kid."

It sucks hearing that name, but I follow her north into the woods, and we begin climbing through some rough terrain. We move slightly eastward, away from the river, Hans galloping like a young wolf through the ash trees, the oaks and hackberry and cedars. Green-covered boulders stand out of last year's leaves. I can't help it, adventure scents the air.

I can still taste her kiss. Okay, maybe I can't, but it's good thinking it. Julie climbs ahead of me, and I can't take my eyes off of her. She moves fluidly and almost silent through the forest. She has rock-climber legs and . . . well . . .

Finally we come to her campsite. She hasn't brought much; one knapsack. We gather up everything and trek back to my camp. It makes me worried that with all my tools and supplies I might be the Roman Empire here; surrounded by barbarian hordes. And later, will dying wraiths struggle out of the city? Starving, wall-eyed people? It sounds cold, but I wonder how many people I'd have to share food with until the food ran out.

I think I have a pretty dramatic mind. Maybe that's okay for times like these. Having never met Julie's boyfriend, I hate his guts. He was probably playing football when the stadium lights went out. Hans is tickled pink that Julie is bringing her stuff to our campsite. He dances all around her like an idiot. I'm scared, and it has nothing to do with the Dark Plague. That's what they called it, remember? When it began happening. I remember Anderson Cooper talking about the Dark Plague; before all news shows suddenly died. I'm not scared about what I knew was going to happen.

I'm scared of a girl. I don't lie to myself, and I won't lie to you. She's moving in with me—in a way—and I'm nervous. I have a tendency to get nervous, but it doesn't last long. I won't act like a wuss around her. When she wants to go back there and see what happened and try to find her boyfriend, so be it and good luck. She knows. I knew it a long time ago, I sensed it, I felt it.

We get back to Camp Dylan and lock her stuff in the camper. She hasn't got very many clothes. I have plenty, but she's going to have to do some serious altering; I'm six foot 170, and she's maybe 5 foot 4, a muscular elf. We don't say a lot. She seems as embarrassed and nervous as I am. Hans is all slobbery excited, and he seems to like Julie better than me, I don't know why. I'm the one who's been feeding him.

I take up my camp spade and the .22. "We should get a small project done. You'll probably want to come along."

"Where?"

"We might want to dig something for you, out there in the trees," I say.

"Dig what for me?"

"A—well, a latrine."

"Oh."

"Mine's that way, to the north. No sink or bathtub. The tile's peeling."

"Okay." She laughs. "I'll take the spade and *I'll* pick out the spot."

Working together breaks the tension, I think. We find a fallen log. I dub the spot (not out loud), Julie's Bathroom. I adjust the army spade to make a pick and I chop into the loam next to the log; Julie uses the long spade to scoop dirt off to the side.

Soon, we hear the sound of a truck crawling up the trail from the road that ends about two miles from here. It moves very slow, and I hear squeaks and rattles and roars as the driver navigates the boulder skulls that litter the trail. Julie and I look at one another.

"I think they might be pulling a trailer," I say.

"What does that mean?"

"Well, it might mean that they've brought a lot of supplies; and they're planning to stay here awhile."

We get back to the latrine dig, pausing every minute or so to listen to the truck. When we work, we seem to be in perfect sync, and I think that's cool. The driver of the distant truck knows what he's doing. Very slow in 4-wheel low, gear one, gun it only when you have to, and don't veer off the trail. Finally the truck sound passes the trail to our camp, and I can breathe again. By the time the latrine's dug, the truck has crept off toward Echo Lake. I wonder if we could somehow camo our trail; but would that only draw attention?

We return to camp, and this time Julie makes the MREs. I'm the designated water-fetcher. It's good knowing I no longer have to leave the camp unguarded. I go down to the river and get water. I haul it back; I feed Hans, and sit back in my Grandma Moses chair. I think about that truck and possible trailer. Julie has made coffee, and I accept a cup gratefully. Her coffee is better than mine.

She's watching me. "That chair doesn't look very comfortable, Dylan."

"My first try. What's for dinner?"

She sits down in the aluminum chair. "Salisbury steak, mashed potatoes and peas for you; ham, scalloped potatoes and corn for me. God bless the military. Where'd you get all of these meals?"

"Olie's. It's—was—a survival store. They're expensive. I bought them by the case."

"Yeah." She keeps cocking her head to the northeast. "That truck went to Echo Lake."

"It sounds like it did," I say.

"Maybe they'll form a Mad Max community there."

Or start killing each other, I don't say. "There may be a lot of off-roaders coming here. I'm pretty sure the vast majority of the folks are still in the city. These are probably survivalist types."

"Doomsday Preppers, like you." She gives me a dry smile.

"Hey, it's not like we were wrong—is it?"

"I hope you're wrong. I pray . . ." She looks to the northeast and sips her coffee. "No, that's a lie. I haven't prayed for a long time."

We eat supper, letting Hans lick the aftermath. No sound of the truck and trailer; they must have made it to the lake. They might already be forming an organized community there. People who would probably know the latest on what's happening. I don't want to take the chance joining them, and Julie Really doesn't. The MREs alone cost me half of my parent's insurance policy. God help me, I don't think it's a good time to start sharing.

Evening draws down the black curtain. The quiet forest looms around us, and we listen to the river tumbling over her rocks. Frogs chirp down on the river. Julie is staring at the southeast. "There's smoke," she says. "Somebody finally started a campfire."

A thread of smoke rising from the lake. Flickers of dancing yellow light. "That might be a good sign," I say. Then we both jump in terror as the sound of a machine gun echoes dull in the distance.

I finally break the silence: "That was a ways away."

"That was an automatic rifle!"

"Sounded like it."

We sit in the darkening evening and listen. More gunfire reaches us from the mountain valley. I'm pretty sure this one is a shotgun. I'm glad Julie's here, although since that kiss she hasn't shown me any particular affection. I think she's glad to be here. We listen for sounds of more gun fire, but it grows quiet.

"We can do laundry tomorrow," I say to break the tension, make the night safe again.

"Maybe they've already started hunting," she says. "Both those shots came from the direction of the lake."

"Probably." I don't ask her what they would hunt with a machine gun. "They sounded far enough away."

We've agreed on sleeping arrangements, to my disadvantage: Julie gets the tent and I get the camper. When night falls we go to bed, Hans choosing Julie and the tent. I lay alone listening to the forest night, trying not to think about tomorrow. I'm more worried about her leaving than them arriving. I had thought to maybe at least visit one of their camps for news of the outside world; maybe it would be bad enough to get Julie to stay.

Now, after the gunfire, I don't think I want to pay any visits.

EIGHT . . .

The next day, three more trucks drive up the trail. One gets stuck, and we hear some guy bellowing out curses. It takes a couple of tense hours before the engine moves off again and becomes a distant growl. They're all going to Echo Lake. Julie and I are working together to try and build a crude table out of ash branches and rope. I think it helps ease Julie's nerves. Keep alert, but keep doing things. Work, I believe, is very good for the nerves. Survival 101.

It must be near noon when we hear the gunfire again. This time it's two different rifles, and the occasional bellow of a shotgun, and this time it goes on for a good fifteen minutes. Hans growls at the racket echoing from the lake. Julie gives me a look and goes back to forming our table. It's likely, I think as I listen, that the gunfire is coming from at least two locations. It goes on—"Pop, pop, pop boom!"—until the machine gun goes off, blasting a good ten seconds. Then the quiet settles. Julie's hands are shaking too bad to tie the rope around the table. We've fashioned straight branches into a tabletop, and tied ash legs together. We keep listening. The silence continues.

"That sounded like a mini-war," she says at last. "I had planned on going there, Echo Lake, where I could take a bath, swim. Try to catch fish."

"It's a good fishing lake," I say. "Trout, walleye . . . I'm glad you didn't."

"So am I."

We take the fishing rods down to the river and within two hours we have 12 nice blue gills. While I'm fileting them on the stone, Julie climbs back to watch camp. I'm afraid that people are going to really pour in here, some of them with maybe less than what Julie brought. And we have so much. I think about all those cases of MREs, the tools and rope I brought up here. I take the filets up to camp. Julie has put away the fishing gear, and she's just had a shower. I probably smell like fish guts, but there's not enough sun left to heat the water for a second shower. So? It's not like she's going to kiss me again. There's just enough sun to bake the fish filets, which I bake with a cornmeal coat in aluminum foil. I wonder how many of the 'campers' out there have aluminum foil. It's important enough that I reuse it.

I help Julie fold up and store the shower. She seems calm, and that makes me calm. Tonight we'll eat fish and sunflower seeds, powdered potatoes. We both seem upbeat that we're saving the MREs, a habit we should get into. She seems less—fatal—than she has been. Maybe she's starting to forget the boyfriend from the old days; probably not.

We share the baked fish with Hans. Tomorrow we'll do laundry; then I'll have Julie go through my clothes to see what she can do with some of them. It feels good to not be alone. We finish supper and clean up camp. Another day falls down the river valley. I think that, very slowly, we're starting to adjust to the life here. We both know that the only thing to do now is survive as best we can, and wait.

"What are you thinking about, Dylan?"

I look at the ground. "I think you know."

"When I kissed you."

"I know, it was just a friendly older sister kiss. I won't make some big deal of it. You have a boyfriend." I bite my tongue.

I should not have said that. Julie stares away across the river valley. Her face crinkles. "Yes, I do."

"I'm sorry I said that."

"Why are you sorry?"

I stare into the stars. The night sky is too black; but suddenly I don't care. If this is the beginning of the end, so be it. I always knew it would happen. I didn't want to know; I was through with it. Now I want to know. Before, I decided not to bring any media crap here; I did not want to know. Now, I wish I'd brought solar batteries and . . . .

I look over at Julie: "You have a Tablet!"

She returns my stare. She has arrogant guilt all over her face. "We watched a movie on it, remember? Your first date."

"And that means you've been up to date on everything! You know what's going on out there! You've been doing the CNN short-wave radio thing from day one."

She avoids my eyes. "I know what I've been told, that's all. Things are still functioning, but not for long. Things are going to hell, but right now it's slow. There's a lot of hope—"

"You didn't tell me! Jeez, I wouldn't have minded checking out the national news. It's probably scarier than Terminator Six. A lot of Hurricane Katrina Super Dome hope. But I want to know! It could be a little important."

"The national news is over."

"So what good is that thing?" I hadn't noticed that she keeps the Tablet in a flat pouch on her left hip; I always noticed the holstered pistol she carries on her right hip.

"There are still some connections out there," she says. "Probably not for long."

"You knew I wanted some information. I was going to go to the damn lake to find out things!"

"I'm sorry. I didn't want you to know. I'm sorry. You've trusted me, I should have trusted you."

"Damn . . . well, I was stupid not to know. Maybe I've been stupid all along."

"I'm sorry. I don't think you should go to the lake."

"Hmmm. You're sorry. So now you have to pay me back."

"What do you mean?" She's studying me. She doesn't look all that sorry.

"You kissed me; now I should kiss you." (I'm not Shakespeare).

She smiles. "You're losing your painful shyness fast. You can kiss me on the lips, Dylan. But we're not going to do any heavy making out; so don't get your hopes up."

I take her into my arms and kiss her. Soon enough we're making out heavy in the wooded dark. She trembles against me, and I have the moments of my life. I don't tell her I'm crazy in love with her; you know I am. I don't want to freak her out by going all Norman Bates. But I can die here and now in her arms, tasting her mouth. I hope while she's kissing me she's not just fantasizing about her boyfriend.

I don't complain. I sleep next to her tonight in the tent. Sometime in the night we both wake up hearing gunfire.

NINE . . .

It's about eight a.m., I figure. A hazy morning sky that warns of rain. I climb up to the camp with six blue gill filets and one small bass. Julie is sitting on the camp chair, a pile of my blue jeans next to her. She has my needle and thread kit, and a pair of scissors.

"What's up?" I ask stupidly. "You're making a wardrobe—good."

She gives me her neutral look. "You said I could have some."

"As many as you want." I set up the camp stove and get out the cornmeal. I've thought about seeing if any vegetables around here are edible—wild mushrooms and asparagus, maybe; berries if I can find them. I'm tempted to break out an MRE, but Julie says that fresh fish and powdered potatoes is a good breakfast. I'm sharing my vitamins with her; that must mean something. All those months when I was preparing, in the back of my mind I always worried that I was missing something vital to survival.

Now I know what it was. I look over at her, and she is the most beautiful thing I've ever seen.

"Did you hear the rifle?" she asks, snipping apart my Levis.

"Yeah. It sounded like the 30.06. Only one shot."

"Maybe that's all he needed."

"You kind of always look on the dark side, don't you?"

She smiles at me. "I think it's getting brighter."

As the fish bakes, I mix up the tasteless potatoes and add two little plastic sacks of tartar sauce. Who knows? Then I glass the woods around us. This isn't the season to hear a lot of gunfire. The clouds are forming in the west, and I know that a storm is coming in. Julie is staring off at the western clouds. Thinking of her lost boyfriend?

I slouch into my ash chair as if it's a super-sofa. "So when did you plan to let me in on what's going on?"

"There seems to be a lot more hope out there than I thought there'd be. People are staying calm; but panic is building; that's the elephant between the lines. The only signals I can get talk about any day now it's coming back. It went out before, it'll come back again. Right now, government experts are just investigating—and then it'll come back. People are staying calm, most of them in their homes . . ."

"Wait'll they get hungry," I say.

She gives me a look. Her face is adorable when she's mad. "You don't know that! You don't know anything about what happened—no one does. Now who's looking on the dark side?"

"I guess it's me, this time."

Okay, I make her laugh. "It happened before," she says. "And then everything came back." She looks at me and we both smile. "I guess my life's over anyway," she says. "I made out with a sixteen year old boy. That makes me a cougar."

"I think of you more as a bobcat. And 18 doesn't make you a grown up."

"At any rate, I think the ones driving in here are dooms day preppers."

"Like me," I say.

"And I think maybe their thing is, leave me alone and I'll leave you alone—that kind of thing."

"Some of them, maybe. Most of them . . . maybe."

Julie stops her altering and stares at the gathering clouds in the west. Then we both jump at the sound of the damn machine gun echoing out of the canyon.

"Oh, God!" Julie says. "What the hell is he shooting at!"

"I don't know."

"Echo Lake," she says. "There's got to be something bad going on there. Don't you think?"

"I don't know."

I help her alter the blue jeans. She knows how to sew with a needle and thread, which surprises me. She's copped some of my tee shirts, but she likes them baggy anyway, so she's going to leave them alone. She gutted my sock collection. She took one of my adjustable Cornhusker caps . . .

It feels good working with her, doing something to take my mind away. Something in my hands to work with, rather than thumbing a video game. I hope she feels it too, the pleasure of raw organic old-school work. It seems to help her cope. It does me.

The machine gun again, making us both pause. It's not getting closer; it's still coming from Echo Lake. Now the booms of the .12 gauge shotgun. When I went to shop at Olies, sometimes I'd meet a real wacko survivalist, with Armageddon eyes.

"It's gonna be the old days come back," they'd say. "You mess with my goods, it's gonna be the old days, Brother. I'll shoot you before you blink."

Had reality released the insanity they'd lived for so many years? Was this their chance to kill people and not be punished? I'd believed and not believed that it would happen, and that I had to prepare for it. Some of these guys at Olie's were as hard as you get. They more than believed it would happen—they wanted it to happen. They adapted me as a son and tried to recruit me. I couldn't imagine surviving with them. They were hard, almost feral characters, pouring the useless money into camping gear and knives and guns. One old tree bark confessed to me that he had 50 guns, and in his fantasy he'd kill the last man to try and steal his last jerky.

None of them would probably go to Echo Lake; they would go into deep country and savor their victory over the skeptics and nay-sayers. They wouldn't be crap-blasting a machine gun—I think. That guy's using up a lot of ammo.

"Hey, sixteen year old teen-age boy," Julie says, breaking me out of my stare. "You look like you're deep in thought about something. You can borrow my tablet, if you can find anything out there. Just remember to charge the batteries."

I smile at her. "I'm just thinking about . . . our neighbors."

She frowns. "What about them?"

"The machine gun—I think they're just warning people to stay away from them. Same with the shotgun. I don't think anybody's killing anyone over there."

"As long as they stay away from us," she says.

Hans is becoming the Great Forest Dog. He scampers into the woods, and too often we have to wander out and hiss him back. We don't raise our voices. We sit and work on Julie's new wardrobe. At about five o'clock we hear them snaking up the trail; it sounds like a whole convoy of trucks. We hear voices yelling, angry curses. The sound of maybe ten trucks crawling up the bouldered trail. The woods are quiet, as if even the trees are listening. The convoy grinds past our path and on up the trail toward Echo Lake. It's more racket than we've heard in days, and we're both on edge.

"Maybe it's a Baptist summer camp," Julie says.

I break out laughing, although there's nothing to laugh about. I lean over and give Julie a hug, and soon enough we're kissing. We put the sewing kit and blue jeans away. In the west the rain is beginning, falling in lavender curtains. We storm up the camp, and when the rain comes we crawl into the tent.

"I have a battery light," I say.

"No," she says, snuggling up to me. "I'm getting used to the dark."

TEN . . .

This morning we hear gunfire just as the sun is coming up. We crawl out of the tent and listen. This time it goes on for two hours. I'm thinking it's coming from three different locations. We slog around the muddy campsite. It's too cloudy to use the camp stove or to break out MREs, so we eat a dismal breakfast of saltines and trail mix. It's a gloomy morning, and the unending racket of guns makes us sour and depressed. I keep my .22 close. It sounds like a damn war out there.

"They're wasting a lot of ammunition," I remark.

"There's got to be something wrong," Julie says.

The gunfire won't seem to end. We get out my two big plastic tubs and while Julie is filling one with water and detergent, I tack a clothesline to two trees. The gunfire pops and booms over the hills. We decided this is laundry day. Hans doesn't like the racket from over the hills. I don't think he's gun shy; I think he's upset because we are. We load the dirty clothes into the soap tub and wash them the pioneer way. I put clean water into the rinse tub, and we get the job done as best we can.

Did I mention taking clothes pins? The plastic ones, they're lighter. I have about 100 plastic clothes pins. I think inventory when I'm nervous. I guess thinking of the goods I've brought here gives me some confidence in my abilities.

The storm pulls a white veil of clouds behind it, but the sun finally comes out. The gunfire has stopped. After all that, the silence seems more menacing. I'll be glad when the camp dries out. We get out MREs (eggs, bacon and hash browns for both of us). We open the solar grill to the wonderful sun and start a pot of coffee. We eat breakfast and clean off our home-made table. I approach her and take her into my arms and let her tremble against me.

"God, Dylan," she whispers. "What in God's name happened?"

"I wish I knew. Anyway, it sounds like the war's over—for now."

"It's going to get worse. Don't try to tell me that it's going to get better any time soon. You're a survival nerd, you've studied this scenario. All this stuff you have, you carefully planned for this—so you know this."

"I don't think anybody knows this," I say.

"Tell me it's not going to get worse."

I look into her face and it's hard to breathe. It's like nothing else around us is really happening. I've never been in love before—I had no idea how powerful it is. I take her face into my hands.

"I think, Julie, that, it might get a lot worse."

We're very mindful of the woods around us. Sporadic gunfire startles the hills all afternoon. Julie is proud to have a good chunk of my butchered wardrobe for her own. We spend a lot of time hugging today, kissing, trying to comfort one another. It's early evening when we hear a caravan of 4-wheelers roar up the main trail. They pass by our side trail, and we relax. No, we don't relax.

"The ones who come here on those," Julie says, "are probably going to be desperate."

"Soon enough," I agree. "They passed us by."

She gets quiet for a long time. She stares down at the river. She gives me an intense look all at once. "Do you want to go with me on a long hike tomorrow?"

"Yeah . . . I guess. A long hike where?"

"To the highway."

"Thirteen miles," I say. I don't like her plan.

"Twenty-six. We have to get back. Why are you squidging your face up at me?"

"Well, it's a day's trek. We'd have to leave the camp alone for a whole day."

"Okay, I'll go alone."

"No, you won't. I'll go with you. But what do you think you're going to find at the highway?"

"People."

"They probably won't be friendly people."

"I want to see, Dylan."

I take her into my arms and kiss her. "We'll see together."

We set out at dawn and walk the bouldered trail down to where it meets the dead end dirt road, about three miles from our camp. It's a beautiful spring morning, everything smelling fresh from the storm. We don't talk or make any noise, and we're mindful of any sound of a vehicle approaching. Hans is on a leash, and he doesn't like it.

This is a pretty gnarly trail; rocky, steep and infested with ancient tree roots. A county road to the south takes the easy way to Echo Lake, but we haven't heard any trucks roll in from that direction; I think the bridge must be out. I feel a little Daniel Booneish with my rifle slung over my shoulder. Julie, of course, has her pistol strapped to her hip. That's probably the sexiest thing I've ever seen. We have trail mix and two canteens of water, and we both took a vitamin pill. (Don't forget canteens).

We make it to the dirt road. All's quiet, not a whisper of humans. We don't want to meet anybody, but it's a lot easier than going cross-country, and we'll have to use the bridge to cross the river. Besides, cross-country could get us lost. I want to get to Highway 31, see what's there and get back to our camp as soon as possible. Walking this dirt road, I feel exposed, vulnerable. We have two articles that would be very valuable; a pistol and a rifle.

Not until we reach the bridge do we see anything; then we come upon an abandoned car, a Honda Civic. I wonder where the guy thought he was going to go with that. I wonder where the driver is. We cross the Kitawki on the steel bridge and take a break under a giant oak tree near the road. Now we're on gravel all the way to the highway. We eat trail mix and drink from the canteens. The world seems strangely empty.

We're about to go on, when Julie grabs my arm. Three people come walking up the road from the direction of the highway. I shouldn't say they're walking; they're shuffling, heads to the ground. The tall guy looks to be in his forties, the woman who follows might be his wife; then a boy of about 10 or so. A family, probably. They move like the walking dead; like starving refugees. The man carries a pistol.

I wrap my hand around Hans' big mouth and we sit tight under the tree. The three refugees don't seem to know where they're going. This road will only dead end at the forest. They all look down with dead eyes, even the boy. We watch them straggle down the road to the bridge.

"They're not even carrying a knapsack," I whisper to Julie. "They look hungry."

"The guy is carrying a gun," she says.

We don't see any more people until we reach the highway. We conceal ourselves in a mess of bushes and look out at a very disturbing scene: many cars litter the concrete. Some cars and SUVs roar past, not stopping for anything. People stagger down the highway, carrying back packs. They move instinctively in groups. Why is this happening so fast? I had expected empty, nothing highway.

Some of them speak, trying to take charge; but most say nothing. They just wander south down Highway 31. We see thousands of people in the distance; abandoned cars and materials. Some bodies lie by the side of the highway, probably dead. This must be what catastrophe looks like in the Middle East and Africa, when refugees wander toward some kind of hope. This can't be happening so fast. Is something chasing them out of the city?

"Where are they going?" Julie whispers to me.

"I don't know—probably nowhere. They figure a highway must lead to something."

"Look at how many!" She stares down the highway. It almost looks like a living carpet, the way it moves with people. Each time a car or truck rolls past, desperate people try to grab onto it; they yell with hoarse voices. We hear gunfire; then Julie takes my hand.

"I've seen enough," she says. "Let's go back."

"Good idea."

We only see a few people on the way back. Like all the others, they seem dazed, as if trying to wake up from a bad dream. We avoid them; then as we approach the bridge, a middle-aged man appears from under the concrete abutments. He's ragged, spent and un-showered. He doesn't have a gun. He's dressed in khakis and he's hefting a back pack. He's in his fifties or so.

We're startled; and immediately Julie pulls her pistol. The man studies us for a few seconds; a gentle smile grows on his face.

"Don't worry," he says to us. "I'm about as harmless as it gets."

"We're coming from the highway," I say.

"Yes. So am I. I used to camp here in Abraham. Don't worry I won't bother you. Don't you have any gear? Supplies? Food?"

"We just want to be left alone," Julie says.

"I'll leave you alone," the man says. "I want to be alone too. You look like high school students. Where are—did you attend school?"

A very weird question, considering. "I went to Holmes," I say.

"Ah, Holmes; a very good school. Where did you attend, young lady?"

"I graduated from Southeast. I was planning to go to Eastridge College."

"Oh. Do—did you decide your major?"

"No," she says. "What difference does it make now?"

49

The man looks away at the trees. "I'm not sure. I'm a high school teacher at Fairmont. I teach math."

I'm studying him. "Do you have any idea how this happened?"

"No. I have a theory; but it's a crazy one."

"We've got to be on our way," Julie says.

He gives us a sad smile. "Of course. I'll say my goodbyes and wish you good speed and luck."

"What's your theory?" I ask.

"Oh, it's—a little crazy. I've been watching contrails. I haven't seen any out here, but near the city they're everywhere."

"Contrails."

"Do you know what they are?"

"The trails jet airplanes send out," Julie says.

"Yes. In this case, there are contrails; but there are no jets."

"I don't quite get you," I say. "What does that have to do with this?"

"I'm not sure. Maybe nothing."

The math teacher returns to his spot under the bridge, and we hurry across the river. I think it's probably best to stay away from people for the time being. I think most of them will be like that guy; stunned, half-insane, trying to wake up. We don't run across any other refugees, and in the late evening, we make it to our camp. We look it over and take inventory; thank God nothing is missing. There's enough sun left to cook two MREs (fried chicken, mashed potatoes and corn). We're both starving and, taking our meal at our home made table, we're quiet. Julie keeps glancing at the skies.

"Well, we went to the highway," I say. "Doesn't look good. I thought we'd see an empty stretch of concrete. I never expected to see . . ."

"I didn't think it would be that bad. It doesn't make sense: that many people wouldn't just pull up and start going down a highway. Not yet; it's too soon."

"I don't know. But I think you're right. I didn't think we'd see anybody on Highway 31. Something really doesn't make sense."

I wish I'd talked a little longer with the math teacher; at the time it hadn't seemed wise.

We finish our supper and brush our teeth. Julie wanders to her forest bathroom, and I sit petting Hans. I've never seen any contrails around here. Contrails without jets? Hmmm. But I know that a catastrophe like this might bring out the crazy in people. I've thought about it a long time, believe it or not. I used to write down in my notebook end-of-the-world scenarios, and how they would play out, and how I could survive them. I made lists for nuclear attack, gamma ray burst, super-virus, economic collapse, fast global climate change. Sad to say, it pretty much dominated my life; hence the lack of a girlfriend. I put myself to sleep imagining how it would be; I jawed for hours with the survivalists who gathered at Olie's. When the first black-out hit and lasted 36 hours, I felt exhilarated; the sense of a great adventure tickled my spine.

I told you before that I always knew this would happen; but I lied. I'm sorry, but I never once thought that it would really happen for good.

I was one of those losers who obsessed on the internet with other losers. We were all getting prepared for the quick downfall of man; but at least I considered it a fantasy, like Dungeons and Dragons. Then my mom and dad made a suicide pact and carried it out. After that, I knew something was coming. I was not as creepy as some of the trogs who hung out at Olie's, but I began to get close. I spent my weekends camping in the woods outside the city limits. I tried to memorize plants that were safe to eat, and those that weren't. Like some of the Olie's guys, I was starting to have visions, and I was terrified that I would go insane.

Now I'm glad I was that way. The math teacher under the bridge, he couldn't hope to survive out here. I think he'll stay under that bridge until he's a skeleton. What we saw at the highway is only the beginning. Very few people truly prepared for this. When it started happening, and it hinted that it would finally happen, a lot of folks said they'd rather be dead than live in . . .

Julie wanders back into camp and sits down in the aluminum chair. We walked 26 miles today, and we're both exhausted. I smile at her; and I think that I'd rather be alive with her, no matter how bad it gets; but I'd rather not live without her. I know I'm only 16, and these feelings are weird. I don't care, let them be weird.

"Do you still want to go back?" I ask her. "If you do, I'll go with you."

She smiles at me. "No. But thank you. I saw enough."

"I think we're better off than . . ." I gaze away.

"I snooped through all of your goods," she says. "When you were down fishing the other day."

"Oh?"

"Two heavy boxes of nails. What for?"

"Hammers and nails are important. How do you think we put this table together? How did we get our clothesline?"

"I'm glad I found you," she says, putting a thrill in me. "I don't know where I'd be right now."

"I'm glad I found you," I say.

We watch the sun fall down across the river. I'm glad we went to the highway—and I'm not glad. We could have brought the old math teacher with us, given him food, saved him. It didn't seem like he wanted to be saved; but how many of those poor folks wandering down Highway 31 toward Sanville would kill us for our food? They're not going to find salvation in Sanville; they're not going to find it anywhere.

"Were you a cheerleader?" I ask Julie.

She gives me a hard look. "You know the rule: no talk about the past."

"Yeah, all right. I'm sorry, that was a stupid thing to ask you."

"Yes, I was a cheerleader."

"Okay. No more past." I gaze at the darkening sky. Contrails can linger on after the jet's over the horizon. You see a contrail and no jet, so what? The math teacher's eyes were very intense when he said that about them. "Have you seen any contrails, Julie?"

She looks at me. "Not that I know of. He was crazy, Dylan. What would contrails have to do with anything? Those people we saw—those people walking down that highway—every one of them has some crazy Hollywood theory. It's because they're scared. And I'm scared!"

Hans thumps up to her, worried. Julie rubs him and cries, trying not to. She's like me, a silent crier; one who fights it. Did she think she might see Him, her lost love, straggling down that highway? People are already flowing out of the city, in cars until the gas is gone; on foot. I'm surprised. How could it be happening so fast? I wanted to know the truth. I didn't want to hike to the highway, and now I know why.

"Are you okay?" I ask her.

Julie sniffs herself dry and rubs Hans, who thumps tail and grins, and hasn't got the slightest idea what's going on. That's ironic, because neither do we.

"Dylan, I would have shot that guy, if . . ."

"The math teacher," I say. "It might have been for the best. He didn't seem all that ready to survive."

"Maybe he thought it's not worth it to survive," Julie says. "Not anymore."

"That's ridiculous. I thought you climbed rocks for fun. Why did you do that? The challenge—the danger—flipping the bird to the world. If it's not worth it, why didn't you just toss yourself off a mountain and get it over with?"

"I don't know." Julie stares away. "Those people; the ones lying by the side of the highway . . ."

"They might have been sleeping, resting."

"Dylan, they were dead! And everybody just walked and drove on past them like they were fallen logs or something."

It's getting dark and we're both very tired. Hans is sleeping hard now, snoring as if everything's well and good. His legs twitch at a dream, and we both smile at him. I need a good hot shower, but that will have to come tomorrow. Our lives are very dependent on the sun right now. We haven't heard any gunfire since we returned. Maybe we'll begin to understand how lucky we are, having the tent and all of those military rations; the truck and camper for storage. The tools and implements and ammunition. Most important, we have each other.

It's a quiet night. We see lightning, but it's far south of us. Here the sky is clear, a sparkling jacket of stars. "Still too black," Julie says. "You want to watch a movie?"

"Sure."

She sets up her Tablet and we watch a classic: Shrek XII, with the sound turned down low. Some parts of it make Julie laugh, and it's good to hear that. Tomorrow is shower day, and she already got dibs on first. That means I'll be doing some fishing. We crawl into the cedar-covered tent and fall asleep together. In the best way we can, we are planning for the future.

Eleven . . .

More gunfire this morning; it's getting to be predictable, like an alarm clock.

Julie makes breakfast. I take Hans and the .22 and do a wide patrol of the woods around us. I think this might be a good way to start the days. I keep thinking of all those people wandering down Highway 31; and that it can't be happening so fast. They would hunker down and stay in their homes for maybe months, only leaving to barter, then to scavenge, then to steal. But that would be a long process. I'm sure every human around is already thinking of winter. Even that wouldn't have driven so many of them out of the city, so soon.

The echoing "Pops!" are rifle bullets. I don't hear the machine gun or the shotguns. Then I hear a loud "Crack!", and I'm sure it came from a .38 pistol. We eat breakfast and listen to the sporadic noise. Hans is already halfway through his dog food, so he's going to have to get used to fresh fish. We clean up camp. Julie prepares for her shower, and I climb down to the river with Hans. There are some big catfish in the Kitawki, and I think that, after another storm, I'll dig up some night crawlers and go after them. Supplement the diet and all that. As it is, I only catch blue gill.

It's late morning when Hans and I climb back up to camp, where we discover Julie sitting having coffee with an older woman in jeans and flannels. Hans growls, but thumps up to her friendly. I have to stand and stare for a moment.

"Dylan, this is Margaret," Julie introduces. "She didn't know we had a camp here."

"Uh . . . Margaret . . . hello . . ."

"A good camp it is," Margaret says. "You've got it covered up. I just stumbled in here by accident; I was trying to find out who was blasting those damn guns."

"We don't know," Julie says, pouring me a cup of coffee. "It sounds like they're all around Echo Lake."

"My ears are practically useless," Margaret says.

I'm studying her, without being rude. She might be in her 60's, with iron-colored hair and tired wrinkles. Not a zomboid from the city. She has a wicked-looking pistol strapped to her jeans, a Beretta from the look of it. She sits comfortably, as if she were in a parlor.

"Margaret's been living in this forest for five years," Julie says.

"Good Lord. How?"

"I started out camping," Margaret explains. "Then in the winter I began moving into one of the ranger cabins back there where the camper station is—used to be. I'd drive to Sanville once every few months to get supplies. I've got a beast of a Dodge Ram pickup; it's out of gas now. But I stocked up. I've probably got more than you kids have."

"So, you don't know what's happening," I say.

"Sure I do. People are pouring in here shooting machine guns. And I don't want to have anything to do with them. I was surprised to find you two here."

"We're not being very social," Julie says.

"Good. You stay that way," Margaret says. She's petting Hans on the back. "This one reminds me of Rusty. He was a Shepard mix; my best friend, Old Rusty. He just died last winter." She brushes away a tear and sighs at the woods. "One day I woke up, and he just died."

"I'm sorry," Julie says.

"You won't have to worry about me coming around to bother you. About what's happening: you know and I know that's it's going to get worse. All you kids need to do right now is survive. Somewhere down the road it might start getting better. I've seen some of the people coming in here to the woods: they're scared.

Maybe they camped here before, or they're trying to get away from others; until you kids, I haven't seen one who looks like he can survive a year out here."

She reminds me of my grandmother, who hated technology: Cell phones, video games, texting, twittering, computer dating, blogs, You Tube, Net Flix, Blue Ray, television, My Space, Face Book. My grandmother hated all of that; and she was tough, like this old woman. She had a farm in Nebraska we used to visit. I remember Grandma growing string beans and tomatoes and cucumbers, and preserving them in Ball jars, in brine . . .

"Care to join us for dinner?" I ask. "Fresh baked blue gill."

"No, thank you, I have to get back. Don't worry about me, I've got plenty. But if you don't mind, I'd like to come visit now and then, check up on you. Now that I know you kids are here."

"That would be great," Julie says.

Margaret gets up from the aluminum chair; Julie gets up from the ash chair. I want to be sociable, but I can't wait to get a shower. We say our goodbyes and she disappears into the forest.

"That was a little weird," I say.

"I got out of the shower," Julie says. "And she's standing there. I thought she was a ghost at first. She had no idea we were here until she wandered up our trail. She was as shocked as I was. She reminds me of my grandmother."

"Mine too."

"I'm glad she found us; I'm glad."

"She seems nice enough. If she's been out here for five years, she could be a very handy friend. I need to fill the shower; I'm pretty grubby."

"I filled it for you," Julie says. "And I'll start the fish."

I pour another cup of coffee and consider how many people we've witnessed in the last couple of days. Margaret was by far the least creepy. We hear no gunfire out there; the woods are quiet and sunny. Hans falls asleep in the shade of the big sycamore tree that looms over our site. It gives me some kind of peace, staring up at the sycamore tree, as if it was the one on my grandma's farm, so long ago. Julie takes the .22 and goes on a 45 minute patrol while I get a blessed shower and put on clean shorts, jeans and tee shirt. I powder my boots with Arm and Hammer soda (don't forget five boxes of it).

I hear a faint rumbling coming from the trail, a mile or so north. Then Julie comes sprinting into camp, Hans hot on her trail. She's carrying the binoculars.

"You'd better come see this," she says.

I follow her into the woods and we climb up the rise to the main trail. The rumbling sound is getting slowly louder, and I know that some major movement is going on. She hands me the binoculars.

"That clear area there, ¾ of a mile or so."

I take up the glasses. Big trucks are crawling up the trail, bearing heavy construction equipment. Bobcats, front end loaders, a bulldozer. Leading the way is a big Caterpillar. Trucks bearing tools and supplies make up the end of the great snake. None of them are military.

We make a hiding place in the trees, and Julie holds onto Hans. A few minutes later, the Caterpillar crawls past; then a jeep carrying two men and two women, all bearing what look like Ak 47's. Then the equipment trucks and the rest. In the beds of the trucks are two riflemen scanning the woods east and west. We're crouched down, peering through leaves and branches.

"What the hell is this?" I say.

"It's construction equipment. All of the workers have guns."

"I noticed. What the hell are they going to build around here?"

We lay there watching the convoy grind past and head off to Echo Lake. Eight large trucks, major heavy equipment, one armed jeep, four big pickups and the Caterpillar pulling fiberglass supply trailers. Maybe forty men and women. They all ride in the pickup beds, and they all carry rifles. I spot some children, and two dogs (Pit Bulls, I think).

Finally the roar eases down into the valley northeast of us. I put down the binoculars and give Julie a squeeze on the leg. "Mega-survivalists," I guess.

"Anybody you know?" she asks.

"I don't think so. They're not military—or government. Looks like they're on their way to the lake."

We hike back down to camp. It would have been a sign of hope, maybe, a crew of people and machines that size moving in. But there was the thing about all those rifles. I had scanned what faces I could, and I didn't recognize any of them. They were all hard, scared faces.

I know that there were survival groups just outside the city that had formed miniature armies for the end of the world. People who obsessively hoarded gasoline, water, guns and food. Was this one of them? They seemed pretty organized. Was it a colony in the making? What did they plan to construct? Why were they here?

We eat dinner in silence, sharing our fish with Hans. Evening creeps into the woods. The roar of the convey quiets down and a very spooky stillness hangs in the air.

Julie sits on the aluminum chair and stares down at the river, wearing her sour, depressed face. I don't know what I can do to cheer her up. She acts like she wants to be left alone, so I visit my bathroom and on the way back I pick her some wildflowers. That's not lame, is it?

She's sitting there petting Hans, her eyes very faraway and sad. I know about the time of the month when girls would rather be left alone. Was that it? Or was it what the old woman Margaret had said, that things are going to get a lot worse. I give her the flowers and her face brightens.

"Thank you, Dylan."

I see that she's been crying, and I look away into the evening woods. I've never been much of a crier. I cried when my mom and dad died; and my pet cat Felix. A few other times, but not many to speak of. I know that I don't like seeing Julie cry. Maybe it's good that civilization is already arriving here; but I wonder what kind of civilization it might turn out to be. I always pretended what it would be like if things fell apart. I figured it would come down to one-day-at-a-timing it. And if it never happened, I might have wound up in some isolated cabin in Alaska or somewhere, still pretending.

But what we saw at the highway freaked me out. What do other highways across America look like? I won't lie to you, I'm scared. Julie's right: those people lying in the ditches are dead. It's happening, I understand that; but why is it happening so fast? Those people are dead. They might have been next door neighbors—but they're dead.

"Were you a football player?" she asks me out of the blue.

"Yeah. Third string. Freshman team."

"Not bad."

"Yes, it is bad. One step away from the water boy."

She laughs. "I'll stop being a wimp. Sometimes girls get to cry; that's the rule."

"I don't blame you for crying," I say. "I'll bet there a lot of folks crying out there."

Suddenly gunfire chatters over the southeast hills. The damn machine gun. Only this time automatic fire erupts from several locations. We listen to it interrupting the dark quiet; then Julie says, "Let's sit on the ground."

We sit on the grass at the edge of our site and hold each other. Julie is trembling all over; I'm numb. Automatic rifle fire dominates the dark. Hans whines at the gunfire and tries to get into our laps. It's a lie, of course, that I'm numb. I feel her body close to me, her hair tickling my neck. I have the utterly weird thought at this moment that maybe I'd better start shaving; I have a sandpaper chin. Truly, I could die right now, it feels so good holding her, stroking her long hair, feeling her against me.

"When are they going to shut up!" she cries at last, making me flinch. "Is it a war, or what?"

I hold her in my arms. "They're wasting a lot of ammo," I say. "Maybe tomorrow you can stay here in camp, and I'll hike over there—"

"What!"

"Just to see what's going on. I'll be like an Indian; they won't see me."

"That's crazy, Dylan. You have a rabbit gun; they have high-powered machine guns. Listen to that!"

"They won't see me." I take her face into my hands and kiss her. Her lips taste salty, like tears. Then she burrows her head in my shoulder. "We really should become aware of what's going on around us," I say. "The crazy old lady of the hills found us; other people might find us. We might need to know, Julie."

She kisses me, and I feel hollow in my stomach. I wish she was in love with me, but what are the odds of that? I don't know. I mean, we've done some heavy—what my parents used to say—petting. Hugging and kissing. But there might be some truly macho guys out there, ex-marines, ex-football players. Older guys with some experience being around girls.

It's time for bed, and we take Hans into the tent and curl up in our separate places. The machine gun fire has stopped. No moon, and it's pitch black outside. Julie comes over and puts her sleeping bag next to mine. She lies down next to me, and touches me on the arm.

"I'll go with you," she whispers.

TWELVE . . .

I don't like the idea of taking Hans with us; but we can't just tie him up in camp. I don't like the idea of Julie going with me. There might be trigger-happy yahoos prowling all around the lake. We eat an early breakfast of saltines, trail mix and sunflower seeds. This will be a much shorter trip than the one to Highway 31, but it'll definitely have to be cross country. We take our weapons, of course, our canteens and the binoculars (buy the best field glasses you can afford, and practice with them).

We set out at sunrise, moving through the quiet forest. The tall hill northeast of us is mostly pine and cedar. It's a good hike to the top, and when we get there we can see Echo Lake shining like a blue mirror about a quarter mile away. We take our break here, and I climb up into a pine tree with the binoculars.

It looks kind of like a military camp. The bulldozer that came in yesterday is already being used to do something. I can see tiny people moving all about, setting up camps. I see campsites all around the perimeter of the lake. Campfires are sending up grey smoke. I very slowly glass the forests around the lake, and spot several sentries with rifles. There are probably numerous camps down there, none of them trusting the other. It's been long enough that some are probably beginning to run out of food. The lake is surrounded by fishermen. I spot the big Caterpillar sitting like a yellow dinosaur. South of the lake I can hear gunfire from the woods. No real signs of warfare.

I climb down from the tree and give Julie my report. She's sitting on the pine-needle ground keeping Hans quiet. My altered blue jeans look good on her. Julie's eyes are very intense, speculative. All told, she seems pretty rested compared to me. The climb up this hill has made my legs burn; but she's used to climbing cliff faces. When she cries, she seems vulnerable and a little weak. I have to remind myself that I'm the weak one; I'm not as tough as her, and maybe not as tough as Margaret. There might be some seriously tough individuals down there at the lake.

"I don't think we should go down there, Dylan," she says. "They probably don't want us down there."

"I agree. Maybe they're trying to set up some kind of refuge for people; but refugees are hungry. They won't want to be sharing a lot of their food. I hate to admit it, but I don't really want to share ours."

"Have you seen enough?"

"I don't know what I saw; but I've seen enough."

"Let's go back home," Julie says.

We hike back to our camp and take inventory. No footprints, no theft. I don't want Julie to be sad, but she's sad. Hans curls up on the soft grass and falls asleep. I love Julie more than my life. I'm a 16 year old wimp. I admit it—I am clueless. You can plan all of your young life; but you can never plan for this.

I look at Julie. "How do you think of me?" I ask her. "I mean, What do you think of me?"

She gives me a startled look: "You're a great guy, Dylan. You're only 16 years old, and you're amazing. What do you want me to say?"

"I know what I want you to say; I won't ask you to say it."

"I'm scared, Dylan." She gives me a savage look. "I've been scared for too long! I've never been scared like this, where it never stops! I can't get into some romance thing."

"Some romance thing. With a 16 year old," I say. "I kind of thought we were already into a romance thing."

She changes the subject: "Could you see what they're building over there?"

"Not really. I think the convoy that moved in yesterday is going to be like the alpha colony. They have to have had some deep pockets; but what are they going to do when their gasoline runs out?"

"Why would they come here?"

"I don't know. Maybe they're a survivalist group that scoped out Echo Lake a long time ago. It's isolated, it's a source of fresh water near the river; it's in a bowl and protected. The land around the lake is fertile enough to set up gardening. They had to have planned to bring machines and supplies in there; and I think they're going to bring more stuff there."

We decide to have an MRE lunch. We heat up Swedish meatballs for me and a fish-and-chips meal for Julie. We'll share with Hans. We make several trips down to the river for water. No sound of gunfire yet; maybe this new group has brought some law and order. We have lunch and clean up camp.

"At least we're staying in shape," I say.

Julie smiles at me. "You're a stud," she says.

That pretty much blows up my heart. All that I have lived for is in this moment. Maybe you have never really felt love. I don't know. All I know is—it's everything.

"I love you," I say.

"I love you," she says.

Some time in mid-afternoon Hans growls and barks, and the two men with machine guns stride into our camp.

They're dressed in camos, and they look at me and my puny .22 with some contempt. I don't like the way they study Julie. One guy is short and a little pudgy; but his partner is tall and burly, and looks ex-military. We say nothing as he looks around our campsite, and chuckles at Hans, who growls and tries his best to look menacing.

Finally Julie breaks the silence: "You guys want some coffee?"

The big marine smiles at her. "Yeah, that'll be fine." He looks at me. He has dead eyes. "I'd put that popgun down, kid."

The pudgy guy has his AK trained at me. I lower my .22, but I don't put it down. I think we're about to get robbed, or worse.

"We're just camping here," I say to the marine. "Are you guys camping at the lake?"

He doesn't answer me. I have a bad feeling about this guy. This is probably a guy who'd served in the military and had a hard time adjusting to civilization. So now that this is all happening, he thinks he's in his element. Maybe he is. I'm a scared teen-age wuss in his eyes.

The pudgy guy finds our hidden camper and spreads apart the cedar branches. "They got this thing pretty loaded up, Scotch," he says to his partner.

Scotch, the marine, nods and studies me. "You know what's going on out there, boy?"

I look at Julie. She's making coffee in the solar oven. She knows this isn't going to go down good. "Hans, be quiet!" she says. She gives me a fearful look.

"We're not sure," I say to Scotch. "What do you know?"

Scotch sits down in the aluminum camp chair and lights a cigarette. I think he might have a Rambo thing going. I've seen guys like him at Olie's; tough and feral, wanting to be a dominant creature at the end of days. I'm not that different. The pudgy guy is probably one who played survival games on his computer; he's having a Boy Scout adventure at last, with a tough marine to lead him. This thing that is happening to the world is very exciting to these guys. I don't like the way Scotch keeps glancing at Julie.

She gives Scotch a cup of coffee, and he grins at her like a dog. "We found you!"

"We just want to be left alone," she says. "Tell your people out there that we're harmless, and we just want to be left alone."

"I can see you're harmless," Scotch says. "I can see that your boyfriend—fuzz-chin here—is harmless."

He grins at me, and I act the wimp, blinking my eyes and looking fearfully at the ground. The pudgy guy takes a cup of coffee from Julie and leers at her. She gives me a hard look, and I know that this is going to get bad.

"I don't want coffee," Scotch says, looking at Julie. "I think I'll escort this young lady into that tent you got hidden there. Billy, you can keep the kid company until I'm through; then you can have your turn."

Billy smiles like a pig. He looks at Julie: "You're hot," he says. "You're sleeping bag stuff."

"Thank you." Julie looks at me. Then at Scotch. "I don't want to be escorted anywhere," she says.

His eyes are hard. Hans growls up to him, and he kicks the puppy away. "I didn't ask you what you wanted. Stand still, Boy!" he orders me. "Don't try anything, boy. It's burning out there, I seen it. Everything's burning out there. This ain't a video game anymore. I'm stomp-tough, and I'll eat your balls out of your skull."

"Okay." I hold up my hands. "We don't want any trouble. We're peaceful."

"We want to be left alone," Julie says.

"I want you to show me your tent," Scotch says. His eyes are completely animal as he looks at Julie. It's the end of the world, and he wants to release his evil. He wants to empty his nuts. He glances at me like a demon. "Your girlfriend is going to show me the tent. And then she's going to show Billy the tent. And you're going to sit here and be a good boy. Okay?"

I look at Julie. "Okay," I tell him.

"You don't want to die; do you?"

"No Sir, I don't." I've been watching the cigarette in his hand. I flinch as Billy grabs Julie and kisses her grossly on the neck. She looks at me calmly and blinks her eyes.

"You'll like it, Bitch," Billy slobbers at her. Julie nods to me, and it's time.

I snap the safety off my .22, raise it, and when he drops his cigarette and steps it out, I shoot Scotch in the head. He stares at me like a zombie and I shoot him again. Then I swing the rifle over to Billy, who is deer-in-the-headlights. Julie jerks her pistol out of the holster and shoots Billy straight in the face. Hans is barking like hell. We stand looking down at two corpses, people we killed. I don't know what I feel at this moment; everything is fuzzy and not real. I look at Julie.

"Self-defense," she says. "It was self-defense."

"Yeah." I look down at the two dead men. I'm glad Scotch is dead, because he scared hell out of me. He had to be killed. In my old fantasies, I imagined men who had to be killed at the end of the world. Those who turned into animals and raped and robbed and murdered. Julie is watching me.

"My God—what did we do?" she says.

"We'll have to drag these guys away," I say. "Somebody might look for them."

"They were going to rape me." Julie gives me a horrified look. "They wanted to rape me!"

"And we killed them." I shake my head at the sky, not believing what had just happened. "We'll have to get rid of these bodies. That's all we need to do right now. I'll do it."

"No, I'll help you."

We take Scotch's field knife and his AK; we take Billy's AK and four clips of ammunition. We drag their bodies down and toss them into the river, and they float away. I wonder who's going to come looking for them.

We go back to camp and pretend that nothing had happened. Hans trots around the camp, upset and anxious. There's not much to say. I ask Julie if she's hungry, and she's not.

"There might be others," I say. "They might find us, like those guys did."

"I know." Julie stares away. "They won't leave us alone, will they?"

"I don't know." I go to her and put my arms around her. We tremble against each other. I kiss her and press her against me. "They would have killed us," I whisper to her.

"I know," she says against me. "But we killed them instead."

"We did." I kiss her.

It's an awkward evening, and we don't speak much. We sit listening to the dusk. Gunfire from the direction of the lake rattles our nerves. Finally Julie wanders off to her bathroom. I think she maybe goes off to cry in private. I see faint lightning far to the west, and the smudge of rain clouds. I guess Scotch and pudgy Billy showed us what's out there. I try to get the images out of my brain, how it was when I shot Scotch; the stupefied look on his face. It wasn't something I had calculated; I just did it. I'm not sorry I did it.

I'm examining the two Ak 47s when Hans growls and stands alert. He's learning how to guard our site; I wish he'd learn faster.

"It's just me, don't shoot." Margaret comes up our trail and into camp. She bends down to pet Hans. I give her the aluminum chair. It's too late to use the solar oven, so I can't make coffee. I had thought of building a campfire the other day. After today, I don't think so. "Where's Julie?" she asks.

"She's using the bathroom. She's been gone awhile." I look into the darkening woods.

"Thought I heard gunfire from over here, and I figured I'd check on you."

"Yeah. We shot a couple of rounds . . . target practice."

Margaret looks at the blood stains on the ground that we'd forgotten to cover. "Oh, target practice."

"Have you found out anything about our neighbors at the lake?"

"No; I stay away from there. A new family moved into one of the ranger cabins. They have some supplies, and they're friendly. Scared, of course. A young man, his wife and a girl of about ten."

I'm just about to go check on Julie when she comes into camp. She smiles at Margaret and I give her the ash chair. Her eyes are red from crying.

"You okay, Honey?" Margaret asks.

"Yeah."

"The folks I've met up here have been friendly." Margaret looks at the blood stains. "Some of them will get desperate by and by."

Julie stares away at the nightfall. "We killed two men today," she says.

The three of us are quiet for several moments. Finally Margaret says, "I heard the gunfire. I was getting some firewood . . ."

"They would have killed us," Julie says. "We killed them."

"Well, these days you gotta do what you gotta do. I might end up killing a few."

"They would have killed us," Julie says to the ground.

"I know. I'm sorry, Honey. There are probably some bad ones down there to the lake." The silence is too much for her, and Margaret finally gets up. We remain uncomfortably mute. "I'll be heading back. You kids be careful."

"Thanks, Margaret," I say. "We will."

When Margaret's gone we sit quiet, Julie petting Hans. It's sinking in, what we had to do. There's no use talking about it. I worry about Julie; I worry about what might happen; whether we'll have any kind of future. Finally Julie breaks the silence:

"I'm homesick," she says. "I want to wake up from this and be home!"

"You called this place home the other day."

"It's just . . . Dylan, it's just that it would be hard enough living like this and knowing there's no going back. Why do we have to be terrorized? I can't believe—what we did!"

"We had to. I'm sorry, Julie . . . what do you want me to say?"

"You can't say anything, Dylan. You're an end-of-the-worlder, like those guys—"

"Whoa. You're comparing me to them?"

"No, I'm not. But you've had fantasies about—about what is. You've thought of shooting people, haven't you?"

"Yes, I admit it. This is what it is. Hey, you shot the fat guy. It's not like you were Little Miss Fainting Barbie or something."

She looks at me for a long time; then she laughs, and that breaks the tension. We both laugh as inappropriately as we can. The future might not be okay; but it's okay right now. Hans barks and grins at us, and grabs up his play stick. The terrible pressure is relieved, and we're two teenage kids in a strange new world. It was bad that we had to do what we did; but we're both very relieved that Billy and Scotch are dead. We retire to the tent and lay against each other making out. I try to get handsy, but Julie draws the line. "No prego," she says. "But I will tell you, Dylan."

"Okay . . . what?"

"You're a 16 year old boy; but I love you. What do you think about me?"

"I think you know that." I go to sleep thinking about what she told me.

Thirteen . . .

It rains during the night, a soft patter against the tent. Both Julie and Hans are snoring. I lie awake and listen to the rain. I wonder why the world is falling apart so fast; it hasn't been that long when everything went off. Somehow, this doesn't make sense. It was going down the tubes when I rolled out. I had plans for a Thoreau thing, only in terms of years. Build a cabin, back to nature, escape the digital world. I never thought it would happen; and now, I never thought it would happen this fast. Can humans become animals this fast?

I hear something outside; the sound of boots sloshing past our tent. Hans jumps up and barks. I creep out of the tent with my .22. It's pitch black; the rain has stopped. In a bright stroke of lightning I see a figure, hunched over, alarmed at Hans and his puppy barks. A man wearing a rubber raincoat.

"I've got a gun," I warn him.

"Jesus!" his voice says. "What the hell?"

Julie crawls out of the tent and turns on our battery light. She's holding her pistol. "What do you want here?" she demands of the figure.

"Don't shoot," the man says. "I'm not armed. I didn't think there were people here. Good Lord!"

"What do you want?" I ask him.

"Nothing. I used to camp at this spot, that's all. I didn't know anybody'd be here."

"Where are you camped now?" Julie demands.

"Nowhere. I just came here."

"Why?"

"If you really want to know, I came here to end my life."

We don't say anything to that. The man is probably in his sixties, and he looks crippled and spent. He studies us in curiosity, as if we aren't real.

"You're both very young," he says at last. "Adam and Eve. Maybe there is some hope."

"Did you come from the city?" Julie asks.

"Yes. And I saw them."

"Saw who?" I ask.

"The ones who turned off the grid."

Julie is staring at him. Slouched in his rubber hood and slicker, the old man resembles a wizard, or maybe a troll. "You came here to commit suicide?" she asks.

"Yes, young lady; I'm here to commit suicide. I'll do it down on the river; you won't have to clean up or any of that."

"What do you mean?" I ask. "Who turned off the grid?"

"The ones who chased everybody out of town. Humans are scattering like sheep. Some of them saw them. Some just ran in horror, not thinking about how they're going to survive. I don't want to survive. You're in danger of humans, because they're falling fast. But it wasn't humans who caused this."

"Who are you?" Julie asks.

"Who am I? I was a scientist. I'm now a dead man." He smiles at us in a tragic, ghoulish way. "You're both young. I'm old. I've had enough of it."

"What about them?" I say. "The grid?"

"You're probably scared of other people," the man says. "I've run into bandits, and they took everything I brought; my knapsack, my knife. That's okay; I knew before I drove out of the city that it didn't matter. Everybody's scared. Until you see them, you won't be truly scared."

"What does that mean?" Julie asks. "Who are 'them'?"

"The ones who caused this. You'll probably find out. I hope not. I wish you the best. Goodbye."

"Wait!" He's trying to climb down the muddy slope to the river. Julie holds the battery light up and we see him crawling like a crab around the boulders and trees. I want to grab him and hold him back, but I don't. "Hey, hold on!" I yell. "What are you—"

"Leave him alone, Dylan," Julie says.

The guy disappears into the darkness of the river. Julie and I hold hands, and we listen. Nothing. I wanted to ask this guy about—about what?

"He was old," Julie says. She shuts off the light and we're in the total blackness of the night. "He could barely walk."

"I wonder what he meant about 'them'."

"The ones who caused this." Julie stares at the blackness that falls down to the river. We can hear the river flowing in the night. "You don't know anything about that?"

"No."

"Who's responsible? Who caused this? No conspiracy theories?"

"No, Julie; I don't."

"Do you think he just killed himself?"

"I think he did," I say. "He was old; maybe he was just at the end. He scared the crap out of me slogging in like that, after the rain."

Julie hugs me and puts her face into my neck. "Is there something scarier out there than all these crazy people?"

"I don't know. I wish I'd asked him about the contrails."

"That's probably crazy," she says against my neck. "Don't go weird on me, Dylan."

"Hey, I think I've done okay so far."

Her voice is strange in the black night: "Do you have a really strange feeling about why this is happening so fast?"

"Yeah, I do."

Julie ventures up to the edge of the hill and looks down at the sound of the river. Then she comes back and I hold her in my arms. She smells of the dense forest. I kiss her salty neck. It's so dark that we can barely see one another.

"What in God's name is happening, Dylan!" she says.

"I don't know."

We go back to sleep in the tent. I think the strange guy has gone down the river. I wonder what is happening out there. I lay with Julie and Hans in the sleeping bags. I remember the day when I knew this would happen; when it all went off and nobody could explain how, or why. Terrorists? Gamma ray burst? Sun spots? Batteries work, cars still work. Nothing else works.

I touch Julie as she's sleeping. Thank God I found her. It must have been God who brought her to me. There must be God.

We wake to gun fire, but it's getting to be a daily thing. Machine gun fire that disturbs the morning air. Already trucks grind up the trail, bringing supplies to Echo Lake.

"Be quiet, Hans!" Julie says.

"More neighbors," I say. "You look beautiful this morning."

She smiles. "You look like a dorky 16 year old boy."

"Is that bad, 18 year old stuck-up girl?"

"No. It's not that bad."

We both go down to fish this morning. No sign of the guy in the raincoat. He must be far down the river by now—literally. We can only catch blue gill; that's getting pretty old. Julie takes Hans up to camp, leaving me to fillet our lunch. It feels good cleaning the fish on this old flat stone that stands against the river. I climb up to our camp, where Julie is giving Hans a shower. It's comical, and I can't help but smile.

"I needed to," Julie says. "He stinks."

"Oh, Hans," I say. "You have to stay clean."

Hans wriggles and shakes, and Julie laughs, washing him down. "You're such a good pup. You good pup."

The days are getting warmer, and I'm glad I chose this place. We get a steady wind from the west that blows up from the river. Summer will be a bit brutal, but it will be better than winter. This winter I'll do a lot of hunting. Deer, wild turkeys, hogs. Every day I regret not having a shotgun and a supply of shells.

This afternoon we climb down and go for a swim in the river. The water is cold and fresh. This is a small cove in the river where I used to swim. Julie wears a pair of her hiking shorts and one of my tee shirts. I brought swimming trunks with me (Don't forget them). It's wonderful being in the water, floating under the sun as the river rushes past us.

It's about 3 o'clock when we get out of the water and climb back to our camp. We're both hungry, and we open two guilty MREs to the blazing sun (beef stew and bread). I put up the clothesline to dry our swimming stuff; we change clothes, make coffee and relax in the shade. I think this evening I'll make another ash chair for Margaret. Julie is relaxed, and she seems happy. Exercise makes her happy, so we'll probably be spending a lot of time swimming this summer.

But we both have that strange guy in our minds. I think he was probably over-dosing on something when he staggered into our camp. Then he waded into the river and finally passed out. It was what he said about 'them', the ones who'd caused this; the ones who shut down the grid. Not human?

"Hey, Sweet Sixteen." Julie's smiling at me. "Your face crimps up when you're worried about something."

"I'm trying to figure out who 'They' are. What that guy said."

"He was on drugs or something. He was just crazy, like the contrail guy, the teacher."

We hear sporadic gunfire in the distance. Hans sniffs the cooking MREs and rows his tail in the air. The sun beats down merciless, but there's a thankful breeze blowing from the west, where Highway 31 is. How many people are dying under this sun? Struggling along that concrete ribbon until they just fall and the heat stops their lives. It's just early summer, and it's going to get hotter. No air conditioning anymore. Even now I think about what's to come that will be even worse—winter.

A long barrage of gunfire; we listen, and then finally Julie says, "They have to run out of ammo some day."

"You'd think. Maybe they're having a war over there. Julie, there's something not right about all of this that's happening."

"That's kind of a no-brainer, Dylan."

I kiss her pursed lips. "People wouldn't act this way just because they can't turn on lights anymore or watch t.v. Something more is going on here."

"You're the survivalist. Surely you thought about the power grid going down."

"Not like this. If it was a gamma ray burst or a solar flare, they'd know. And it would have happened all at once. How many times did it go out for a couple of days or so. It always came back on; but nobody could explain what had happened. If it was terrorists, they'd know. I just wonder what the guy meant by 'them' chasing people out of town."

"It has to come back on some time. They'll fix it and see what happened, and it'll all go back. This can't be forever."

"I don't know," I say. "When it started to happen, and when nobody could explain why, I knew something very bad was coming."

She snuggles up next to me and shivers herself still. "We killed people, Dylan," she whispers. "What in God's name do we do now?"

"We wait," I say.

FOURTEEN . . .

We're down at the river fishing when the pontoon boat comes down the current. Julie's about fifty yards downstream from me, near our swimming spot. She's casting out a Silver Spoon, hoping to get a bass. The river people don't have their motor going, so we're not aware of them until they come around the bend upstream, and there they are. I never expected to see anybody on the river.

I sit very still, hoping they'll pass by and not see me; but Hans—the fool—starts barking and howling and dancing along the river bank. They look over and see us. It's about a thirty foot pontoon with a crew of three women and three men, all sprouting AKs, all scoping the river banks. They wear uniforms, but not military. Black and white jumpsuits, black and white baseball caps.

I wave and smile at them. They all wear sunglasses, and that makes their faces cold, robot. Hans yelps and bellows at them as they pass, and one of the guys in the boat raises his AK.

"No!" I yell. "He's just a puppy!"

They drift on past me, staring hard. I take up my binoculars and watch the boat drift past Julie. She's hiding in the willow bushes, and I don't think they spotted her. I sit back and wonder what that was all about. I wonder if they're part of the group that seems to be assembling at Echo Lake. I think these were planners. They didn't shoot at me. I suspect that they're part of a strange community. Supplies are beginning to pour into Echo Lake. Something big must be going on there; that's what Julie thinks.

She stumbles up the river and calms Hans down. He's acting like a dufaloid, and that worries me. I adapted him because I fell in love with him. (Take a trained dog, not a puppy).

"Did they see you?" Julie asks me.

"Yeah, they did."

"What kind of goth weirdos were they?"

"I don't know. There's a wide stream that cuts off from the river, about a mile south of here; it's the stream that feeds Echo Lake. They might go down there."

"What the hell were they doing?"

"It looked like they were patrolling the river."

We climb up into camp and put away the fishing gear. We didn't catch any fish, so I set out two MREs in the sun. Pork steak, mashed potatoes and corn. Salisbury steak, baked potato and green beans. I think about the pontoon crew. They're obviously part of a large and organized group. They wore uniforms; they looked military, but they're not military. I wonder about joining them. I'm sure that they have more than we do; it would be some kind of civilization.

We eat lunch, clean up the camp, brush our teeth and fill the tubs for laundry. Julie wears a pair of my sweatpants, and she whishes and twitches as if she's strolling through a cloud. I wish the pontooners hadn't spotted me, but Hans had to open his big mouth; and it nearly got him shot.

"We could join them—if you want to," I say.

Julie looks at me. "Join them."

"I think they're part of the group that's bringing all the equipment in here. They're organized. They're probably going to store a lot of gasoline."

"Gasoline," Julie says. "What's that got to do with anything?"

"It might be a planned society forming at the lake. I don't know. All of the damn trucks coming in here . . . maybe we should check them out."

"They probably know where we are anyway," says Julie.

She looks very cool wearing my over-sized sweats. What if we joined the black-and-white league, and she met a guy her own age? I try to remember the people I saw riding in the pontoon, their sunglasses and rifles aimed at the river banks.

"Why were they in uniforms?" Julie asks.

"I'm not sure. All black and white. Black and white baseball caps. They were all wearing expensive shades."

"So were we." Julie stares off. "What do you know about this? Is it some kind of compound?"

"I think so," I say. "There were some people who dealt at Olie's big time. They didn't want you to know anything about them—we knew they were the mega survivalists. They were the planners of future communities, for when civilization falls. Not the weird scrags like me; people with serious money. I think one group like that planned to go to Echo Lake. Now they're doing it."

"Are they peaceful?"

"Probably. But one guy in that pontoon almost shot Hans."

"I think we should leave them alone," Julie says. "And hope they leave us alone."

I'm relieved that she said that. We don't need them, we have our place here. We rinse our clothes in the freshwater tub and hang them to dry. I'm with Julie, we only want to be left alone.

But near sunset they come into our camp. There are a dozen of them, men and women of various ages but most fairly young; all dressed in the black-and-white sweats, black combat boots, black-and-white ball caps. They carry AKs. Hans barks up to them, and a girl kneels down to pet him.

"It's okay, little boy. Oh, you're a good puppy."

"Hello," Julie says to them.

An older man steps out of the group and looks our campsite over. He's in his sixties, I guess. He wears a wild beard, and he has the haunted eyes of a modern-day prophet. He's dressed as the others, only he wears a gold cross. He studies us with kindly eyes. "We've found you," he says. "And we will save you."

"Save us from what?" Julie glances around at the black-and-white group. We're getting quickly freaked out.

"We've found you," the man says. "We will lead you to the Savior."

"Who are you?" I ask.

The man looks at me and gives me a gentle smile. "My people call me the Judge. Judge McCarthy. Our community is at the Savior's Water."

"Echo Lake?" I say.

"You children will be safe when you join us," the Judge says. "You're not safe here."

"We want to be left alone—for now," Julie says.

I don't like this guy's God-crazy eyes. Behind his gentle smile is something really scary. He studies Julie as his people stand silent, like guardian robots.

"Have you accepted the Savior as your Lord?" He asks her. "Have you accepted the Savior?"

"Yes, I have," Julie says.

He turns his eyes on me. "Young man, have you accepted the Savior?"

"I have, Sir," I say.

"Then you have to join us," Judge McCarthy says. "You'll be protected; you'll be part of a community of God."

"We'll consider it." Julie looks around at the group, their AK 47's.

"You stupid kids." An older girl steps up to us. She's a commando chick, probably in her late twenties. "Don't you know who's popping those caps over there?"

Her outburst startles us. I realize that this "club" is dense with fear. Maybe they're more afraid than we are. They're older than we are; but only the Judge looks older than 30.

"It's a gang." This time a dude steps forward; he looks to be in his mid-twenties, and might have served in the military from his bearing. "A gang of human wolves. We don't know what they call themselfs; they rode in here on 4-wheelers, and they're armed to the nuts."

"We heard them ride in," Julie says.

"We're the good guys in these hills," Combat Chick says. "What do you think they'll do when they find you?"

"Gloria, don't scare them," Judge McCarthy says. He gives us a grandfather smile: "We're here to help you."

"They didn't seem to bring many supplies in," I say.

"That's the problem," Military Dude says. He keeps his sunglasses focused on me. He keeps his head shaved, a good reason to wear the ball cap. I wouldn't want to fight him. "They're the children of Satan."

"They have a lot of ammunition," Gloria speaks up. "And we think they're on meth."

"We have tried to avoid them," Judge McCarthy says. "Others at the Savior's Water are joining us. I know you children are afraid; everyone is afraid. The Savior will protect you. The Savior sent us to save you."

I trade looks with Julie. "We'll think about it," I say. "Thank you for the—offer."

A silence. This doesn't seem to be an acceptable answer. I wonder how long this "club" has been preparing for Armageddon. I don't recognize any of them; but they all wear identical ball caps and shades, and some of them could have dealt with Olie. I might have blogged with some of them; but I never read anybody mentioning Echo Lake—or, the Savior's Water. They might be a religious end-of-the-world cult, there are plenty of them out there. For all their lock-step grimness, they don't seem extremely threatening, not like Billy and Scotch. I wonder if those two were part of this gang they're talking about. They might have been on meth when we shot them, I don't know.

"We're starting to patrol the river, as you know," the Judge says. "Hoping to find and rescue the lost."

"We're not lost," Julie mumbles.

This sets off Gloria, the Commando Chick: "Do you have any idea, Little Girl, what's happening out there?"

They're all darkly amused at this; all but Judge McCarthy.

"The power went out," Julie says. "The electricity—it all went out."

"They don't know anything," Shave Head says. "You guys have no idea. You don't join with us, you ain't going to make it, simple as that. You can hide from humans for a while; but we found you; that means the Satans are going to find you."

"Who are the Satans?" I look at him. "Who are they; the meth-heads?"

"No." He turns to the Judge. "I don't think these two kids are going to help us."

Judge McCarthy has been studying us. I realize that he's the only one not wearing sunglasses, as if maybe they'd hide the power of his eyes. He's what the survival chat rooms called a Puritan; one who for decades deprives himself of all sin, anything that might make him weak on the day of Armageddon. "They are a new generation. Any who wish to join and accept the New World of the Savior, are free to do so; and we would welcome you."

Julie breaks the silence: "We'd have to get our stuff packed."

"You have any gas in that hunker?" Shave-head asks me. "You can pack up your camper and drive on over."

"I don't know," I tell him. "I think she's probably dead empty. I don't really want to try her on the trail."

"You know what kind of equipment we got?" Shave-head says. I find it kind of weird that none of the others in this group are saying anything. They stand with their semi-automatic rifles and look like miniature Terminators.

"We watched you bring it in," I say to him.

I think this Judge McCarthy is the deep pockets behind this. When times started getting scary, he recruited young, healthy survival types, put them through training, filled their minds with the Savior, and gave them an exciting place to belong. Then suddenly, to everyone's surprise, it happened. I'm not much different, except that I never was much of a joiner.

Hans is being friendly, but he's nervous. He sniffs up this group. A couple of the girls give him pets. Julie and I are tense, and that makes him tense.

"We're the good guys," Gloria says. "We're trying to help you."

"We're peaceful," the Judge speaks up. "You must choose to join us, or not. We do not coerce."

"We appreciate that," I say. For a peaceful religious group, they look suspiciously para-military.

"Will you come join us at the Savior's Water?" asks the Judge.

"We probably will, Sir. We want to think it over."

He gives his group a nod. "We will leave you children—we'll be praying for you."

As the group leaves, Gloria says over her shoulder, "I love your outfit, Little Girl. The Charlie Chaplin look."

"Thank you, Little Woman."

After they march away, we sit quiet in our camp, relieved but worried. Hans starts to whimper, and Julie lets him crawl into her lap.

"Was that good?" Julie finally asks. "Or really bad?"

"I'm not sure. I know that machine gun fire was going off before those 4-wheelers came in. If it is true, a bunch of starving meth-heads wandering around doesn't seem very good."

"Is that some strange religious cult, do you think?"

"I don't know. They're part of the group that came downriver on the pontoon; same black-and-white uniforms; plenty of AKs. I don't really want to join them, unless we have to; what do you say?"

"Hell no," Julie says.

"I don't think you'd get along with Gloria." I smile at her. "We can join them later if we want."

The sun is dying in the western hills. It was a hot day, and the evening breeze feels good. We take down our clean clothes, fold them away, and I take down the clothesline. We clean up and hide our camp. Hans gets a dog biscuit for being good around our 'company'. I only brought two boxes of them, and he doesn't get one very often.

"If it wasn't for you—stupid mutt—they might not have found us," I tell him.

"They scared me," Julie says. "I knew they weren't going to hurt us; but they scared me."

"Strange enough, I think it might be a good thing that they set up over there. As far as neighbors go, I'd rather have religious fanatics than meth-heads."

Julie smiles and comes to me. She gives me a surprise hug and kiss. "You are so cool, Dylan. I can't believe you're just a 16 year old virgin."

That makes me smile; but it stings a little. "You don't know I'm a virgin."

She kisses me. "I think you are."

The woods grow dark; then black. No electric halo is against the clouds. Only the hard prickly stars and the black curtain of forest that surrounds us. I think we're calming down after the encounter with the Savior people. I think about Judge McCarthy's strange eyes. How all of those sunglasses looked at us as if we were lost kids. Maybe we are.

"The Satans," Julie says against my neck. "What do you think the marine guy was talking about?"

"He sounded pretty crazy," I say. "It might seem weird to most people; but the power going out is going to bring the real freak-out. I don't think the Saviors are going to be the last ones we see. For a lot of people, no electricity is going to be the true end of human civilization. This bunch; I think the Judge was probably a very wealthy fanatic, who planned this for decades."

"I'm not worried about the Saviors." Julie stares into the lightless forest. "I'm worried about the Satans."

"People are going to get desperate," I say. "Every day the power doesn't come on, and no one can explain why, people are going to see Satan everywhere."

We hold each other and kiss. Our lips taste salty together, earthy. I'm glad Julie doesn't want to run to them for security and spiritual comfort. I don't think she's a joiner either. It worries me that all this is happening so fast. Sad to say, at one time I made a scenario on my old computer, one that predicted how long society would take to crumble if folks had no electricity. It would be a long time, because folks would believe that the power would come back, and everything would be as it always was. Almost everybody would hunker down in their homes to wait it out. What we saw at Highway 31: this crazy stuff shouldn't be happening so fast. I was always the punk kid at Olie's Survival Store; the one the old-schoolers would pat on the head and give me the gen on survival in the True World. They always called it that; a time when humanity would be forced back into the True World. I knew that it was time to get out; why should it surprise me that the old-schoolers wouldn't know? They probably saw it coming long before I did.

I kiss Julie on the cheek; I stroke her hair. We're sitting on the ground, and Hans wriggles to get into our laps. We could turn on the solar-battery lamp, but I don't mention it. She still keeps the wildflowers I picked for her. She might be falling in love with me, I don't know. I know a lot for my age; I know nothing about girls—women . . .

"Did you think that Gloria was pretty?" she asks me out of the blue.

"I thought she was kind of disturbing," I say. "What did you think about the shave-head guy? We never got his name."

"Mega creepy," Julie says. "What about the Judge?"

I smile. Strike three, Shave-head. "He looks kind of familiar. I think he might have done some really big deals with Olie. He's the leader of—whatever they are."

"And the others just stood there silent, like some Nazi guard."

I kiss her. "Why would I think Gloria was pretty? She was holding an AK 47 on us."

Julie laughs against my mouth. "I think we're doing okay on our own for now."

"We are."

Hans follows us into the tent. We'll probably both have a hard time falling asleep tonight. We curl up and lay quiet against one another. We listen to the darkness. We don't talk about the raging gang of meth-heads. We don't talk about the Satans.

FIFTEEN . . .

Margaret visits us this morning. We ate an early breakfast of oatmeal (don't forget a few cases of dry oatmeal), powdered milk and pancakes (a few cases of pancake mix). Hans likes the pancakes well enough.

Margaret sets aside her walking stick and takes the aluminum chair. We've made coffee, and we take a break from our work getting ready for the rain that's boiling in the west, across the river.

"It's going to pour down here pretty soon." Julie glances at the fierce lightning in the western storm clouds. "You'd better watch yourself, Maggie."

"I've been rained on before." Margaret gives us a stern look; as if she's the Woman of the Woods: "You met the religious crazies."

"They spotted us while they were patrolling the river," I say. "Hans opened his fat mouth and they spotted us."

"A few hours later they showed up," Julie says. "Have you met them?"

"Oh, yes. I'm not trying to hide like you kids. They went around to all the cabins up there. I don't blame them for carrying those machine guns. I would too, if I had one."

"They didn't seem hostile," I say.

Margaret is petting Hans. But her eyes stare off. "All these years I've lived up here by myself. I always thought something would happen, sooner or later. I never knew what. Now folks are pouring in here disrupting everything; I told them politely that my religious beliefs are nobody's business."

"So you probably won't join them," I say.

"No. I don't trust them."

"Did they tell you about the meth-heads?" Julie asks.

"They did. If some meth-head gang is out there to the lake, they haven't bothered me. I'm not going to hide from anybody: if they try to kill me and take my goods, I'll try to kill them, and let's see the leavings. I'm not going to live in fear."

Julie looks at me. I know we've been living in fear; and that Margaret knows these woods and this life far better than us. She's lived a life, and now she's a fatalist. I think it might be best for Julie and me to live in fear a little while longer.

"How loud can you whistle?" I ask her.

Margaret gives me a look. "How loud can I whistle? Louder than you, Dylan. When I was a little girl on the farm I learned how to whistle the cows home."

"Let me hear you."

Margaret slips her index fingers into her lips and whistles out a fairly impressive shriek. Julie laughs and slaps her knees. I get up and pour fresh coffee.

"Now you, youngster," Margaret says.

This is stupid, drawing attention to ourselves. Letting everybody a mile away know where our site is. But I want to show off. I put my index fingers into my mouth and blast the air with a whistle that screams down the river valley.

"Damn, Dylan!" Julie says. "Don't do that again!"

Margaret is watching me. "What's the point of that?"

"You know," I say. "If you get in trouble, you whistle as loud as you can. If we hear you whistle, we'll come to see about you."

Margaret sips her coffee. She smiles at me and lets out a weary sigh. "Same for you kids. I'm an old woman, but I won trophies with Polly here." She pats the revolver on her hip. "Isaac Walton Pistol Championships, back before you were born. We had to shoot at moving targets. There wasn't any Girl's League and Boy's League, they threw us in there and the best shot won. I won my fair share with good old Polly."

"Good old Polly is—a Beretta?" I guess.

"Good for you! She's a 16-round Beretta. I can knock the ass out of a jay bird in mid-flight with old Polly."

"What did you think of that Judge guy?" Julie says.

"A handsome man for his age. A nice smile. Don't trust him." Margaret gets up with some moans and groans. She smiles at us. "Babes in the woods. You'd be surprised to know how much I envy you."

"You don't have to go," Julie says.

"I do. It's going to start raining any minute now, and I think it's going to be one of those tree-killers. Goodbye, Julie and Dylan. Don't trust them. The Judge wants to save you and welcome you into his fold. Don't trust him. Don't trust his Flock."

Hans follows her until we have to call him back. Julie is staring at the trail. The storm is forming around us. Lightning bellows far down the river valley.

"Maggie!" Julie calls. "Did they say anything about Satans?"

Margaret's voice from the dark storm: "I already knew about them!"

"What are they!" I call.

"I can't say!" Her voice dies in the woods. "I don't think they're of this earth!"

We scamper into the tent as the kick-ass storm of the year blows in. I love the explosions of lightning, because every time Julie grabs me and hugs me. Rain sweeps in, battering our tent. It gasps in and out as if it's dying of a heart attack. All the while the terrible roar of the rain.

Hans curls in our arms like a child. We lay in one another's arms, and I feel great. All my life I lived a fantasy. A story that took me away from what was real. A girl, a challenge, the greatest adventure of all. A girl, Julie. Nature tearing apart the world as we hold together and listen to it, knowing that it will be gone, and we'll step into a washed world, muddy and ravished; but smelling fresh. Now, here it is. I love storms. I love it because it takes you to the very edge of violent nature. God help me: at this time and in this place and with this girl, I feel more alive than I've ever felt. I feel the danger, I feel the love, I feel the violence of this night. I feel a future of true hardship and tragedy. I don't know why . . . it's just that, when my parents committed suicide, something came to me; at first like a dream, then like a reality. I think I know one thing: what you have at this moment of your life is more precious than you can ever have; because it will never be again. Even at the end of the world.

What did Maggie mean about them being not of this earth? She's as crazy as everybody is now. The two guys we killed, Scotch and Billy; they were crazy. Miranda seems crazy. The Judge is crazy. Are we crazy? When I prepared myself to live like this, it wasn't the world that scared me; the elements. The rain and snow and heat and cold and hungry animals and dangerous humans. Getting food and water and trying to stay clean.

What scared me was going crazy.

"I don't think any meth-heads are going out in that," I whisper.

She laughs and gives me a kiss. "Have you really accepted the Savior?"

"I don't know who he is," I say. "You said that you accepted him—it—whatever. At this time it seems a little stupid to go whacko."

"I was afraid," Julie whispers. "They were all holding guns on us!"

"Yeah." I stroke her hair and kiss her on the cheek. "You think we should scope out another place? Another camp?"

"I do," she says. "It's too dangerous here. Too many people have found us."

"I guess it wouldn't hurt to explore. But damn, this is such a great site. We have everything we need up here."

"Except privacy."

"I don't think they'll bother us; we're not bothering them. Their river patrol spotted us, and they just wanted to check us out."

"I need to tell you, Dylan—this sounds stupid—but yesterday when you were making the rounds, I saw one in the sky."

"One what?"

"A contrail. There, west, across the river."

"No air craft."

"Not that I could see." Julie sighs against me. It feels good holding her and listening to the storm outside the tent.

"You can hear the roar of jets," I say. "They always move just a little bit beyond their trails," she says. "There were no jets. I thought about what the school teacher said, the guy under the bridge. That somehow it means something."

"They weren't clouds?" I ask. "I didn't see them."

"I don't think so. They were thin streaks—they looked very strange. That can't have anything to do with what happened; can it?"

"I don't think so. It all feels kind of like a dream, though— doesn't it?"

"It does. Since it happened I've thought I'm in a dream."

I squeeze her ribs. "A good one?"

"No. But you're making it better."

We lay together making out as the storm rages out there. This is the first time I've ever French kissed a girl, and I shiver. Julie's body is tight and muscular against me; afraid and not afraid. The tent gasps and lashes in the wind. We hear the trees swirl in the wet violence, and we hold each other against it. The world tears itself apart tonight; but we're safe. The tent holds, and we fall into sleep.

We get awake after the monster. The sun comes out fast and hot after the storm. We eat a breakfast of MRE scrambled eggs, bacon and hash browns. The sun is bright this morning, the storm only a memory in the east. We share coffee as the saturated woods drip around us. The storm ripped many branches out of the trees, and I try to think positive:

Fire-wood.

Julie is mad at the muddy floor that was our camp; she hates the sloggy morning air. Hans is in a foul mood; he barks at the woods for no reason and makes a pest of himself. We're all caught up in something that nobody could have predicted. I want to make things better for her, but I don't know how.

She wants a shower, so I take Hans down to the river, sliding down the mud, crawling like a crab with my fishing gear down to the gushing current. The storm really charged the Kitawki; it rages past my flat boulder, and I doubt the fishing will be any good. I climb down to our flat swimming pool, which is gulping huge water from the river. I attach a Silver Spoon onto my leader and try to get a white bass. A great storm like that one can flush fish into a peaceful cove like this.

I do some casts; but my mind isn't on fishing. I keep studying the woods above me. I haven't heard any gunfire. Hans stumbles along the river, sniffing everywhere, like Lewis and Clark. Being in the True World, he's assuming a German Shepard's pride and stature. He seems to be turning into something like a wolf. I hope he never meets a rattle snake.

I know Julie can't imagine living a life like this; not for long. But I can. I'm beginning to love this new existence of forest and river and struggle and danger. I'm beginning to love awful reality. It all smells good; it all feels right. Somehow, I'm stoked to the max. This morning it's as if the storm blew the world clean. I hope Julie doesn't leave. It would be nothing here without her. I'd be some troglodyte eating squirrels and going mad. This is the first time in my life that I ever felt real. How many out there feel the same? To be born from Heaven into the fearful, true Garden of Eden. I hope Julie doesn't leave.

Am I becoming an animal? I glance into the woods. I listen for the sound of that pontoon boat; but I think the river's too wild today. Their camp may have had some major damage in the storm last night. I staked our tent down tight as death in a place that I knew from experience would weather a storm like last night. I'm surprised that I catch three big white bass. They fight hard against the lure, and I take them in slow, not wanting them to spit the lure. I lose six, but I catch three good ones. One fish filet each; me, Julie and Hans; that's premier. I remind myself to dig for night crawlers this morning; then do some serious night time catfishing.

I filet the bass and toss the entrails into the river. The Kitawki; same river that carried Billy and Scotch away. That's a pretty damn dark memory, and it makes copper in my mouth when I think about it. I wonder if the Savior Weirds found the bodies, suspected what happened. The woods are misty; still dripping rain. It's too late in the year to try and build a garden. If we survive that long, we can make a garden next spring. I figure we have enough MREs to last two years, if we go easy on them, which we haven't been. Like everybody—even the hard-core survivalists—the back of our minds is waiting for the power to come back on. For the global sigh of relief. I catch myself glancing at the skies, for signs of contrails. Nothing human could have made this happen, I think.

I climb back up to the camp. Julie is fresh and happy; she gives Hans a big hug, and rubs him. She feeds him a precious biscuit. We hug and kiss and I show off the white bass. The solar oven is spread out, and we bake the fish in cornmeal and aluminum foil. I mix up a batch of instant potatoes. We have a bass lunch with the still-nasty potatoes and trail mix. I have three goals today: to first dig up night crawlers; then to take a shower; then to work with Julie making another ash chair for when Margaret comes around. We don't talk about things that worry us. Meth-head marauders, a God-crazy cult, demons, contrails without jets . . .

We brush our teeth and I make three water trips down to the river and back as Julie tries to dry up camp. We're doing essential work, primitive work. It electrifies me. The danger of the woods electrifies me. I don't know if I ever was happy before; now, I Know I'm happy, watching Julie move around in my blue jeans, cut to her size.

Moving and working and afraid of the forests that surround us, I feel terribly alive. I know Julie is only surviving it out, waiting for the world to come back on. Maybe it will, and all of this will fade back. But right now, I feel terribly alive.

If anybody ever reads this, know that there's a difference between living and existing. I don't want to get all profound;

there's a difference between the world and the earth. While I get my shower, Julie goes out on patrol with the field glasses and my .22.

"There's my sixteen year old boy, all scrubbed up," Julie says, striding back into camp after my shower. "I didn't see anybody out there."

"My eighteen year old girl," I smile. "That's good."

I take Julie into my arms and kiss her. I know that she was out scoping another campsite, one more hidden and safe. But I'm sure the old F-100 wouldn't make it anywhere. I don't really care. Julie is in my arms kissing me, and nothing matters. This is my first and only love, beating her heart against me, breathing against my neck. And I don't give a damn right now if Hell's Angel Demon Release the Kraken Jonestown Zombie Vampire Devils are on the prowl. This is it, at this moment—love . . .

"When it dries up, something will happen," she says in my ear. "That storm—God, Dylan!"

"It was just a storm, and now it's over," I say. I can't tell you how it feels having her in my arms. If anybody out there ever reads this: I hope you'll know how it feels.

"The Satans," Julie says. "The name of a biker gang or something? Bikers who used to come up here . . ."

"I don't think so," I say. "That guy—the Shave-head dude who was checking you out—he said the Satans weren't human."

"The guy's crazy," Julie says. "They're all crazy. Everybody's crazy."

"Except us." We kiss and hug, and I start to explore.

"You're getting feely there, Stud," Julie says, pushing my hand away. "No pregos; that would be very bad."

"You can't blame me for trying."

"No, My Love," Julie says to me. "Someday—but not today."

"Okay. You know I want to."

"So do I," Julie says. "But not today, Dylan."

"I think Commando Chick, Gloria, was checking me out." I give Julie a pinch.

"Ow! You dick; she wasn't checking you out. She's a crazy bitch with an Ak rifle. No, we're not going all the way, My Love. I want to, you want to—but no pregos; not now."

"I'm just trying to be—romantic. That's all."

"I know. And you are." Julie looks away. "Those men we killed . . . there are going to be more—aren't there?"

"Maybe. I don't know. If you want to move, we'll move. But I don't think the pickup will even start. I know it won't unless I could figure a way to charge the battery. And if folks want to find us, they will. This is our place, Julie. It might not be what either one of us planned or dreamed; but it's our place. The world is going crazy, we get that. Crazy people are all around us; and we're camped out in Abraham Forest doing the best we can."

Julie smiles at me. "Sweet Sixteen," she says.

That keeps me pretty stoked for the day. I want to be Mr. Cool around her, but Julie knows I'm no commando. I'm a nerd who got into survival stuff. I might be good at it. But this is more than anything I ever mapped on my computer. I never heard any talk at Olie's about the Satans. Margaret knows what they are; Judge McCarthy knows. The math teacher under the bridge . . . it has something to do with contrails?

We dig into the earth near our campsite and turn up plenty of night crawlers. We spend a lazy day fishing for catfish in the river cove; we don't catch any. Julie is wearing a pair of my altered Levis and one of my red Nebraska tee shirts. Hans snoops along the river, growling at frogs. The forest swings in the wind. We climb up to our camp.

We start to build another chair. This time we cut branches off the sycamore tree right by our camp. We work with the tools, referring to the BACK TO BASICS book; arguing about how the sycamore chair should be made; we don't hear any gunfire. Hans snoops around, waving his tail. The wind blows fast from the west, sweeping the woods.

I stare into the blue sky, and I see it. A contrail, alone in the sky. I look for a jet, a sign of civilization. Nothing, only the wisp of white.

"Look there," I say to Julie.

She studies the contrail. "What does it mean?"

"I don't think one of our jets made that," I say. "But something did."

It's mid-afternoon when we hear the explosion. It comes from Echo Lake, of course. A huge BOOM! That shakes the forest and leaves us stunned.

"My God!" Julie says.

"That was serious ordnance," I say. The woods shudder still. Bird chirps come back. Hans is staring at us with scared eyes. Then the chatter of machine guns from several locations. "The War of the Lake," I say. "Now look behind us at the river."

The pontoon boat drifts quickly past our campsite. Six of the black-and-whites, all sprouting AKs, are scoping out the east side of the Kitawki. They all look very trigger-happy.

"Hans, be quiet!" Julie kneels down to stop his barking.

"They already know we're here." I watch the patrol boat drift out of sight. The heavy machine gunning has stopped, and the forest seems too quiet now, as if it's holding its breath. "I wonder what they're looking for."

"Now we know they have bombs over there." Julie turns away from the river and stares into the trees. "Hans, will you shut up!"

"I know what you're thinking, Julie," I say. "But if we find another place, we'll have to leave the truck and camper behind. Where else are we going to store our stuff?"

"I really wasn't thinking that," Julie says. "I was thinking that maybe we should sneak back up to the lake and do some spying."

"That's a good idea," I say. "I wish that stupid dog would learn when to keep his mouth shut." Hans is smiling at me, wagging his tail, thinking he's getting praise. "First thing tomorrow morning?"

"Don't be too hard on Hansy. There might come a time when we Want him to growl and bark."

Another explosive goes off just at sundown. The forest shakes; Hans runs and hides in the tent. We both stare to the southeast.

"What the hell Is that?" Julie says.

"It could be anhydrous, or plastic, or dynamite. Maybe it's the Savior Weirds doing some construction."

"Weirds?"

"It's what they were called in the chat rooms. The Hand of God coming down and all that."

"And I suppose you could find places that would teach you how to make explosives."

"Yes. I never made a bomb. I figured it would be a waste of time."

We hear a loud grinding noise in the distance from the dead end. We creep up the hill and hide ourselves near the main trail. My stomach rolls at the roar approaching. I clamp Hans' mouth shut.

"What the hell?" Julie says.

A tank rolls around the bend and crawls past. It was military; now it's been stamped with a black and white logo. I don't know what model it is. The logo is a white star in a black circle.

A damn tank.

"The Judge must have been a multi-millionaire," I say. "That'd be a pretty handy thing to have at this time."

"You don't know anything about him?"

"No; I never heard any mention of him."

The tank roars away, and we return to camp. A brilliant sunset colors the west. We sit watching the darkness creep into the woods. We munch Twizzlers and sunflower seeds. The forest grows quiet around us. Julie is trying out the sycamore chair we spent the day building; it's better than the ash one. We've decided to scope out Echo Lake tomorrow morning. In the afternoon we plan to start building a rainwater system of some sort. We both know that keeping busy calms the nerves.

"There's another one," Julie says, looking into the sunset. A white streak. No sound, no sight of an aircraft. "That's not a cloud, Dylan."

"No, it isn't."

Sixteen . . .

Next morning we're studying Echo Lake from a knoll only about a half mile away. It looks like there are two large camps of people, those on the south side and those on the north. The Judge's people are south. I see quite a few black-and-white individuals working on a compound. The earth movers and bobcats are growling away in the woods north of this compound. We hear trees crash down; then the gnarl of chainsaws. Nobody's shooting; but they're obviously building up some sort of fortifications.

I don't like being this close, especially with big-mouth Hans; it's a clear, cloudless morning that already starts to smell like summer. Julie spends a long time scanning with the binoculars. I stare around the woods for signs of trouble. We hear the noise of construction, and some of the Savior people are on guard with their rifles. But it doesn't look especially warlike. I can't shake the premonitions I've been getting and trying to ignore: that something is going to happen. I know, something really big has already happened. But something beyond what I ever imagined, or prepared for.

We're about to leave when Hans scares us with a sharp bark, and goes running into the woods. The Shave-top dude strides out of the trees with his AK. We stare at him; his sunglass-dry smile, looking down at Hans, then up at us. "You guys ain't hiding yourselves too good," he says. "You've got a puppy with you that can't keep its little mouth shut."

"Who are you?" Julie says.

He studies her. He glances at me, then back at Julie. "I'm T.J. Don't get your hopes up; I got a girlfriend already."

"I won't get my hopes up; I've got a boyfriend already."

T.J. gives me a quiet sizing up. "You're right about the 'boy' part."

"Do you want something?" I ask him.

"Yeah. I want you to follow me into Paradise. You might not know it, but you're in Hell now; and I want to take you out of Hell and into Paradise. I'm one of the good guys."

"We're glad of that," Julie says. "It's just that you kind of snuck up on us . . ."

"Imagine if the bad guys had snuck up on you," T.J. says. "Look, why don't you come on down and look our place over. I'm not here to kidnap you; just to try and help you see the light."

T.J. Shave-head isn't wearing his black-and-white uniform. He's in marine camophlage; his face is greased in green and black. Two grenades bulge out of his hips. I hope he's the good guy.

"Just follow me down and meet everybody; we don't force anybody to do anything. Come on down to the Savior's Water and see; then make your own decisions."

"We're just here to see what's going on," Julie says.

"I know; we've been expecting you," T.J. says. "You two kids are a lot more vulnerable than you think. We want to protect you—to save you. But it's your choice. I'm just asking you to come down and meet us. The decision is yours."

I trade looks with Julie. "Protect us from what?" I ask.

T.J. gives me a hopeless look. "You have no idea, do you?"

"No! We don't," Julie says. "Do you know what happened? Who made all of the power go out?"

"If you want to know, then follow me down to the Savior's Water."

T.J. turns and heads back into the woods. Hans growls him away, and we have to get the dog and drag him back. I look at Julie. "He didn't try and take our weapons," I say.

"I don't know, Dylan."

"If they wanted to hurt us, they could have. And they obviously know things that we don't."

"All right. Let's see what they're all about."

We follow T.J.'s path down the rocky hill and into the open sunlight that marks the border of the lake. It's a big lake, five acres or so; I walked around the whole thing once when I was a kid, and it seemed to go forever. It's fed by at least three streams that branch off the Kitawki. Campers are all over the streams, some of them fishing, some washing clothes. They stare at us as we follow T.J. down and into the huge compound that's forming around the north pier of the lake. Many young folks are working, building up earth abutments. Guards with machine guns look across the mile of water to the south shore, where others seem to be scrambling about. It's like a Girl Scouts and Boy Scouts war camp.

Judge McCarthy greets us with his gentle smile. "Welcome, Julie and Dylan!" he says. "We've been expecting you, and we're very glad you came to see us. That goes for Hans."

Hans is barking all over the place, crazy at the human action here. We follow the Judge down to the huge earth abutments. T.J. is with us, and soon enough Gloria, the Commando Chick, comes up. It's a hot day, and the workers—the Savior People—all wear sleeveless vests, black shorts and combat boots. There are a lot of home-made grenades on hips, and survival knives. They all seem cautiously friendly.

We're escorted into a palatial tent full of foam sofas and chairs. A lightweight carbon table has bowls of fruit, vegetables, mixed nuts, cheeses and yogurts . . . we both salivate.

Gloria gives Hans a dog treat. I think he's traitorously in love with her. T.J. grabs a fist of mixed nuts, sits down in one of the chairs and begins crunching. "Dig in," he says.

We sit and politely help ourselves. We're both very hungry, and we eat until we're stuffed. Judge McCarthy is watching us. Gloria and T.J. are watching us. Maybe a better word is 'evaluating'. Outside the tent the sun is brilliant glaring off the lake. Then we hear machine gun fire. A bullet rips into the tent, making us jump and spill the last of our food. Immediately T.J. and Gloria run out with their AKs.

"Come see the bad guys!" T.J. yells at us.

We scamper out of the tent as bullets pop into the dirt around us. We hunker down behind the huge clay battlements the caterpillar dug out. Across the lake there's a lot of yelling and rifle fire. I cradle my helpless little .22, and Julie has her Glock out of the holster, as if it would do any damage at that distance. The Savior kids fire back. There's a long exchange that doesn't seem to do any damage. The lake is too wide for any kind of damage. Both sides seem to be wasting a lot of ammo. Why are they doing this stupid thing? Is this some fear-crazed Bloods and Crips thing?

"Don't waste bullets," I whisper to Julie.

Finally both sides stop, and a relative quiet takes over Echo Lake. This familiar place from my childhood has become a bizarre war zone. Julie grips my hand and we peek over the earthworks. The people on the south side of the lake have what look like foxholes dug out. They don't seem to have nearly the resources as this side. Only some pickup trucks and trailers back in the trees. It's like Desperate Reality Hillbillies or something.

T.J. is really stoked. He grins at us and lights up a cigarette. "The calm after the storm," he says. "Here's reality, Boy Scout."

"Yeah, I get that."

Gloria has been hunkered down with us. Suddenly she rises up and empties a clip at the folks across the lake. Julie holds her ears and stares.

"Jesus! What are you shooting at, you crazy . . . !"

Gloria loads another clip and takes a cigarette from T. J.; I have a feeling they're a—dysfunctional—couple.

I trade looks with Julie. She curls her nose at me. She locks stares with Gloria.

"Gunfire scare you, Barbie?" Gloria asks her. She acts like she's having an orgasm. "Here, have a cigarette; it'll calm your nerves."

"No thanks; it's bad for your health."

Gloria laughs. "Look back there in the woods behind us."

"Your semis," I say, looking back. I'm impressed.

"Hans, be quiet!" I hear Julie say.

Sixty foot trailers are lined up in the protection of the trees. I heard all of them come in, but I'm still surprised they got such behemoths up the main trail.

"Loaded with generators," T.J. says. "Pretty soon we'll have electricity for the whole camp. Across the lake, they got nothing—and they're scared. They're eating their dogs, and we're wiring up for electricity."

"They've got machine guns," I mention.

"Yeah; and every now and then they splatter us, then we splatter them. Time is definitely on our side. In a week, we'll have RPGs in here; and they'll be devil-dust."

"What other weapons do they have?" Julie asks. "We've heard some pretty major explosions."

"That was us," says Gloria. "Now are you thinking about joining?"

Julie peeks over the earth rampart and trains our field glasses across the lake. "Why aren't you inviting them? I think the last thing you want to do is start a war. You're recruiting; why aren't you recruiting them?"

"They started it," T.J. says. "They're non-believers. The day we came here they attacked us. They're dirty and filthy and evil and desperate. The Judge is pretty selective about who he invites. He thinks you'll fit in. We got a lot of stuff; more than you'd believe. And more is coming in. That Bobcat over there in the woods? It's burying a giant gasoline tank. When the meth-heads and low-lifes over there are gone, we'll have the lake to ourselves."

"What if they don't leave?" I say.

"We figure they're already running out of food." Gloria grins at me like a she-wolf. "You look like you want some excitement, Scout Boy."

"Don't you want company?" T.J. asks. "Don't you want electricity? You said you've accepted the Savior as your Lord. The Judge is in contact with the Savior. We're protected."

"We're going to bring in solar panels and wind turbines," Gloria says. "We're already setting up a field hospital in a clearing out there."

I know the clearing. I played there years ago on camping trips. I survey this compound; I admit it's impressive. These young Saviorites are working hard, moving about like pyramid ants. Their first goal, I guess, is to conquer the lake. The look on Gloria's face when she let go with her AK was pure savage animal. Kill the enemy.

Then what? It's pretty obvious that they don't believe civilization is going to get back to normal anytime soon. I see almost no older people around—a few greybeards, but most of the clan is just a little older than we are. That would make sense, I figure, in the New World Planning Judge McCarthy probably spent his life getting ready for: a few very skilled oldsters who had accepted the Judge as the mouth of the Savior; but mostly younger, healthy troops who would follow a Messiah anywhere when the curtain falls over the earth. Fertile breeders of the future. I'd read this in a dozen Sci Fi stories. Never could it have become real, even though the mad side of my brain insisted it would.

"Those folks across the lake," I say to T.J. "Are they the Satans?"

He laughs. "No, Kid. They're trash that washed out of the city. They don't have a chance of surviving. They're dead already."

"Then what are the Satans?" Julie asks.

"You don't want to know, Barbie-girl," says Gloria.

"Yes—Barbie-woman—I Do want to know!"

The Judge walks down and joins us behind the tall earthen walls of his New Jericho. He takes up a very expensive pair of Swiss field glasses and peers for a few moments across the lake. He wears the best Pro Shop field clothes I've ever seen. The tuxedo of survival clothes.

He puts down the binoculars and studies us. "Now you children see what we're doing; and those who want to stop us. Times are very bad, and they will get far worse. The Savior prepared me for this long before you were born. These are times when some should live and make a new generation—and some should not live."

"What right do you have to decide that?" Julie asks.

I cringe. I wish she hadn't said that. In situations like this, I figure it's best to stay silent. I'm as creeped-out as she is; but there's no need, at this moment, to advertise it.

"We don't really know what's going on at this point," I explain to the Judge.

Judge McCarthy gives Julie his spooky smile. "Come and join us, and you will know," he says.

Hans is scared and wants to go home. Ever since Gloria emptied that clip, he's been whining and rubbing up to us. I know these people have full-grown pit bulls roaming the compound; Hans smells them, and he's scared.

Julie rubs the puppy and looks at the Judge. "We've paid our visit," she says. "Right now we want to go back home to our hill."

"Of course," says the Judge. "I'll send some of our people with you to ensure that you aren't molested. Enemies are beginning to filter into the hills."

"No," I say. "I think we'll be okay. But thanks. We appreciate everything."

"Remember this." The Judge fixes me with his prophet eyes: "Many enemies are gathering out there. We are friends."

"Thank you, Sir."

"Dylan . . . you are in far more danger than you know."

Hans is relieved when we trek back into the woods, glancing like deer behind us. Hans stays right with us, and keeps his mouth shut. We climb out of the lake valley and over the tall hill of pines. Julie is very tense, and in mountain-mode. I try to get my mind wrapped around all this. We move softly and continually scan the woods. We're both thinking about what we saw back there; and especially the gunfire.

We take a break in the glade just south of our camp. Julie takes my hand and kisses it. "That was weird enough," she says. "They're going to build a mini New York there."

"Unless the meth-heads get them."

"Meth-heads. You don't really believe that, do you?"

"No." I stare into the woods, rippling softly in the west wind. "They'll have electricity."

"So, you think we should join them?"

"I don't know." I kiss her hand. "It'd be better than dying of no electricity."

"I don't know either," Julie says. "It's tempting; they seem to—kind of—like us, all but Super-Bitch. They have a lot of stuff. But for now, I think we're doing okay on our own."

"Hans didn't seem very comfortable over there. Pit bulls and all that."

We climb down toward the river, and at last we're home. We check out our campsite and find nothing disturbed. It's now early evening. I'm thankful that the sun is behind clouds. We both collapse in camp chairs. We both need showers, but that will have to come tomorrow, if the clouds drift off. I gaze across the river and consider how unprepared I was for this. I prided myself on scoring the highest points in the video survival games. It was my mental world; and then I actually got ready for it. All the supplies I hauled into the F-100; all of the lists I made, and then checked out as I pretended.

It was all teenage pretend. Men like the Judge had seen it before I was born: they prepared knowing it would happen. I never believed it would happen.

"Hey, 16 year old boyfriend." Julie looks at me. "You look kind of zombie."

"Well, that was a pretty intense visit with our neighbors."

Julie laughs. Then her face drops and she stares into the evening trees. "I'm really worried about my parents. When the light comes back in the night, I have to go back there. I know the rule: no talking about the past . . . but I'm worried about my parents."

"I don't think they'd want you to go back," I say. "I don't think the lights are going to come back on."

She gives me an angry look that softens. "We're not supposed to talk about the past."

"Rule Number One," I say.

"But what about your parents, Dylan? Aren't you worried about them?"

"No."

"How they're coping out there—if they're alive? Okay, no talk about that. I'm sorry." Julie takes a deep breath and rubs Hans. "I didn't flirt with T.J. You shouldn't have flirted with that Gloria."

"What? How in the name of God did I flirt with her?"

"When she showed off with her machine gun you were looking at her as if she's Joan of Arc. Her big boobs hugging the machine gun."

"What! Julie, I was scared to death. The last thing to cross my mind was to flirt with her. Anyway; she might flirt with me—in a really disturbing way—but I already have a girlfriend."

I crawl over and begin tickling Julie. She giggles and slams me down with her feet. "Are we going to go crazy?" she asks.

"I don't know," I say. "But that kick really hurt."

"I'm sorry. Let's go to bed, Love."

We crawl into the tent. Hans takes his spot and goes immediately into snore-time. It's not very late, but we're exhausted. We roll up against each other and listen to the still, fragrant night.

"I love you Dylan," she whispers, making me tremble. "I'll go wherever you go."

"You know how much I love you," I say. "I'm not T.J. slam bam—but my grammar is better than his."

She laughs and kisses me. We snuggle in the warm blankets and the quiet night puts us to sleep.

Seventeen . . .

Huge trucks roll up the main trail before sun-up. Julie and I jump awake together and lie there listening to them. Hans growls and whines at us. Outside our tent is the still blackness just before dawn. I feel Julie's muscular body against mine. I'm in pretty good shape; but I'm naturally skinny. I can't explain what it feels like to have her body against mine.

"Sounds like big trucks," I whisper to her. "Maybe they're bringing in gasoline."

"Solar panels and wind turbines," she whispers back. "I want to go home, Dylan. I just want to go back home!"

"I know." I hold her in the dark. The fresh, sinister morning wind sweeps into the tent. Hans gets up and plays the tough guy, standing tall; barking at the sounds of the trucks crawling by, a quarter mile up to the main trail. The Lord Protector of the Camp, a wimp puppy.

"Be quiet, Hans!" Julie hugs and rubs him. The three of us lie together and listen to the sounds of civilization invading our world. I don't want to move, it feels so good with her next to me. I wish the world would just leave us alone. I think that maybe all my parents wanted was to be left alone; but they weren't. I don't think they wanted to leave me alone, but somehow they felt they had to. They loved me; I'm sure of that. They just couldn't go on. I think they saw a world where it was just too hard to go on. But I don't know for sure. Going on means waking up, and getting up, and going back into it as it is. Julie wants to go back home, and if I could, I'd take her back home. I'd take her into the past and erase the future and go on with it. I can't do that.

This might become a savage new world. We murdered two men and dumped them into the river. We're here, on Dylan's Hill. The old world isn't going to come back on. Every night the blackness folds around us. How many are staring at the skies for the glow of electricity? How many have bad dreams, like I do; that it will not come back on for a long time. This is it, for now.

The trucks grind away as we lie here listening. Then suddenly a colossal explosion shakes the earth, and we both freeze in terror.

"Jesus God!" Julie grabs onto me. Hans whimpers and hides in the sleeping bags. My gut rolls; my ears burn, and I get up and scramble out of the tent. On the main trail, a blaze of flame lights the night. Machine gun fire echoes near our camp. I stare at the intense fire and I smell the billows of smoke that welcome the sun of another day.

Julie holds onto me, and we listen to the gunfire. Hans has crept out of the tent, and he's scared. We're all scared. The fire on the main trail is so hot that we feel it waving onto us. It was a gasoline explosion. The gunfire stops, and there's an eerie quiet as the sun rises red in the east. All the woods smell like gasoline. We hear people scrambling over there, yelling and crying. Sporadic gunfire; then it stops.

"They were bringing a truck of gasoline in here," I say. "And somebody blew it up."

"What is this!" Julie says. "Why would there be a war like this?"

"I don't know."

We try to be normal; we open the solar shower so that we can clean up at the end of the day. The trucks have moved on, but there's the smell of gasoline in the air. We get started on our rain-catcher. We hollow out cedar branches for conduits; we carve a big log of cedar into a funnel. We channel it all into the plastic bottles. Each bottle wears a charcoal tab, so the rainwater that soaks in will be pure. If we keep moving and working, that means we're still alive.

We open two MREs (steak and scrambled eggs for me; spaghetti for Julie), and rest on our home made chairs. We hear gunfire in the distance, and Hans whines up to us. Julie pets him; her eyes stare into the woods.

"We can't hide," she says. "My 16 year old boyfriend that I'm in love with. We can't hide."

I smile in spite of myself. "Maybe we don't have to hide."

"Dylan, there's some serious crap going on over there. There's a war going on around us."

"I know."

"And the world out there—God, what is it!"

I take her hand. "It's me and you sitting in a beautiful place, making coffee and watching the afternoon. It's me and you being here and being in love. That's what it is, Julie."

(I'm not Shakespeare)

After our coffee, we clean up camp, and while Julie takes a shower I climb down to fish on the river. I catch nothing. A couple of hours later, Hans and I climb back up to camp. I'm thinking of some way to use rainwater for showers and hygiene. A big cedar-wood shower? It rains a lot here. Rainwater is relatively pure.

Julie smiles at me and shows off the cut-off shorts she made from a pair of my Levis. "It's me and you now," she says. "I guess we'll have to fight the world together."

"I guess." My mind goes numb. "Julie—you're beautiful," I say.

"Thank you. So are you." She smiles at me, and I think that she's as happy as possible. That's all I really want, to make her happy.

I pour water into the solar shower. Gunfire pops out of the south hills. We carve the cedar branches into water tunnels. Julie is quiet. She works with me, pausing to pet Hans, who thumps about nervously. We slice off slivers of cedar wood. We can use the cedar shavings as air fresheners.

"What are we going to do when the food runs out?" she says finally.

I look at her. "There's always food."

"What kind of food?"

"In a pinch—insects," I say. "Worms, beetles, ants—"

"Oh God, Dylan—you are grossing me out."

"I know. They're oogie . . . but they contain high amounts of protein. It's food that can make you survive."

"Eating bugs. Is it going to come down to that?"

"I don't know. Maybe."

"If we join them," Julie says. "If we join the Saviorites—we won't have to end up eating bugs."

"Not at first," I say. "They're super-survivalists. They planned long ago, and they're trying to hold onto civilization. I don't know who the hell is attacking them and blowing up their stuff. I don't know who the Satans are. Nobody ever mentioned them."

"In your survival chat rooms," Julie says.

"Yes. I played all the survival games, and I prepared. But I never prepared for this."

Julie takes my hand. "I can't believe I'm in love with a 16 year old boy."

I smile at her. "I can't believe anything," I say. "But if we have to eat bugs, I get the beetles and you can have the worms."

"God, Dylan. Don't say that."

I creep over and begin tickling her. "Baw—ha ha! Julie will have to eat worms! I will make you eat worms, teenage girlfriend!"

"Stop feeling me up! You little pervert; I'll die before I eat worms."

We kiss, and Hans slobbers up, grinning at us. Julie pets him. "What are you going to do, puppy?" she says. "Find a coyote girlfriend?"

"I've been thinking of how we should conserve our water," I say (I've been rehearsing this speech). "It's pretty important that we—conserve our water, so to speak."

Julie studies me with her deep hazel eyes. "How do we conserve our water?"

"Well . . . mostly in the area of showering. Two separate showers is—wasteful." I don't look at her.

"Dylan . . . no. I'm not going to take a shower with a 16 year old boy. Take our showers together—is that what you're saying?"

"It's the smart thing to do. We don't want to wear the shower out. And it takes a lot of water and a lot of work to . . ." I sneak a look at her. "Okay. Give me points for trying."

Julie laughs. "You *are* my boyfriend," she says.

The black night of this new world falls over our campsite. We both feel fresh, and the air is cool. Julie gives her auburn hair to the west wind. I worry about the gigantic explosion on the main trail. Whoever is fighting the Saviorites must have known a gasoline tanker was coming in here; they must have prepared, and positioned in the trees. They must have planted an explosive on the trail and detonated it when the tanker went past. Then let go with the machine guns. It's as if two armies had been prepared for battle a long time ago. How? There was never anything like this on the Internet, the chat rooms.

Julie glances into the dark woods; and I know that she's thinking what I'm thinking. Even Hans stares alertly into the forest. Strange beings are wandering our woods.

Finally, Julie says, "Why are they fighting?"

"I don't know. It doesn't make sense; not this soon. Maybe later, but not this soon."

"The night is still too black," she says. "I've never seen so many stars."

I don't look at the sky; my eyes take in the black forest around us. Only a quarter of a mile from us they occupy the woods and managed to blow up a gasoline truck. Who are they, and what is their beef? Do they know about us? Our stash of goods?

"Do you think they might be out there?" Julie whispers. "Watching us?"

"I hope not."

"Dylan, I have a bad thing going up my spine."

"I do too."

Eighteen . . .

Margaret comes into our camp with a wild woman who carries an AK. Julie and I get out our fire arms; but Margaret eases us with her hands. "This is Miranda," she says. "Miranda is part of those who've been fighting the Judge's people."

We stare at this new intruder. "Why?" Julie asks.

Miranda stares down at Hans, who is trying to threaten her with his puppy yips and growls. Miranda is probably in her mid-thirties, a grim-looking woman. She's dressed military, all camoed out, her hair in a severe ponytail. I look around, freaked-out. Where are her people?

"What's going on?" Julie says. "Is this a damned war or something?"

Miranda studies us. "You've met the Judge. McCarthy. You've met his cult."

"We've been at his camp," I say. "There was gunfire across the lake, but none of them bothered us."

"You kids didn't know it, but I was watching from the trees when they first came here. You two were scared crapless."

"They didn't do anything," Julie says. "They asked us to join them; that's all."

"Do you know why you're still alive?" Miranda asks.

"What?" I trade looks with Margaret.

"Because you both said you'd accepted the Savior—otherwise, you'd have been killed."

"Come on," I say. "They would have murdered us if we hadn't . . . ?"

"Yes, they would have," Miranda says. "You've never heard of the Judge, of course."

"There was never any mention of him on the survival sites." I'm wondering if this Miranda is crazy. I try to start conditioning myself to crazy people. "Who exactly is he?"

"He's a cult leader. Armageddon, God's wrath, the great final battle between Good and Evil, and He's the one. They're trying to recruit you because you're young and you've accepted his idea of the Savior—and mostly because you're excellent breeding stock. The Judge always thinks about the future." She looks at Julie. "He wants young women to carry his seed into the future." She looks at me. "He doesn't have much use for you."

"How do you know him?" I ask.

"We're all people who believed in and planned for the collapse of society." Miranda gives me a hard eye-balling. "So are you, Dylan; so don't look at me as if I'm stupid. You were in the same world I was, and the Judge—planning for the great sudden collapse. I have a Masters' Degree in Sociology, and you never got through high school; so don't think I'm a delusional idiot."

"I won't," I say. "What can you tell us about him and his—cult?"

"It works this way. Now that everything we planned for has come to pass, this is his Messiah time; what he's been preparing for all his life: the time when only the Believers can inherit the earth. What the earth will be. All non-believers must be culled, so that the Believers can rule. He recruits mostly young people, because he figures they're scared and naïve, and more likely to need a new society of God. Also because young men and women are most likely to survive and fight. And, of course, breed."

"This seems like a pretty stupid time in human history for folks to be fighting each other," I say.

"Is it?"

I hear movement in the forest around us. Hans hears them and lets out his statue-bark. "Who are you people?"

"Survivalists, just like you. Only more mature and experienced and trained, no offense. We came to the Lake first, even though we knew the Judge's people would move in sooner or later."

"Why did you start shooting at them?" Julie asks.

"Is that what they told you?" Miranda gives her a humorless laugh. "Is that what they told you?"

"Yes!."

I'm getting nervous. I know that Miranda's people—whoever they are—have set up in the woods, and are watching us. Julie feels it too, and she has to restrain Hans.

"Your people can come out," Julie says. "We're not violent; we just want to be left alone. If there's some weird war going on over at Echo Lake, we don't want any part of it."

"That's okay with us," Miranda says. "But not with the Cult. We're not wanting to recruit you; we don't want you to join us, because we have too many already. And we don't have nearly the materiel and supplies they do. More is going to come in here. Their first goal is to wipe out everybody in these hills who refuses to join them. That means the time for you kids is running out."

I see Julie shudder. She stares into the dark woods; they're quiet now, but Hans can sense the people out there, crouching in the dark.

"Hans, be quiet!" Julie says. To Miranda: "Are you what they're calling the Satans?"

"No, we're not. We want what you two want, to be left alone. The Cult will not allow that, I'm afraid."

"Your people can come out of the trees," I say. "We're harmless. We don't have AK 47s."

That's a lie, of course, because we have Billy and Scotch's guns.

"I know better than that. They will come out, soon. For now, I'm going back into the trees. Consider this a warning: If you do not join with them, they will kill you."

"It's true," Margaret says. "They saved me from the Saviorites. Miranda saved me; that's why I brought her here."

"Why would they want to kill us?" Julie says. "All of the nightmare crap that's going on—why would they want to kill us?"

"If you don't join them, they will kill you," Miranda says. "I came here to warn you—I've warned you."

"If what you say is true," Julie says. "What can we do about it?"

"I don't know." Miranda gives her a sad, motherly smile. "How old are you, Honey?"

"I'm eighteen," Julie says.

Miranda looks at Margaret, and they walk away into the darkness of the forest. We can just see Miranda's silhouette, and the rifle she carries on her shoulder, when she says, "We'll come to you if we can," she says. "But don't come to us."

"You're on the north side of the lake," I say to her.

"We're everywhere," Miranda says.

"Tell us what the Satans are!" I yell out. They already know where we are. "Tell us about the contrails; we've been seeing more of them."

"Don't worry about that right now," Miranda calls from the dark. "Right now you should look to the earth, not the sky."

They vanish into the darkness, and we sense the others melting away with them. Hans goes quiet and laps his drinking bowl, glancing up to slobber at the woods. I thought I was saving the poor mutt from the pound and probably euthanasia; only to drag him into this, whatever This is.

"Why would they want to kill us?" Julie finally says.

We hold one another in the dark. We're both salty with sweat, and scared.

"Dylan, this should be when everybody gets together to help one another—to save one another!"

"I know. I can't understand why this is happening." I look at Julie: "Did you believe what that Miranda said?"

"I don't know; she seemed crazy. But Margaret seems to trust her. Dylan, there were people out there in the dark, watching us!"

"I know. This is not anything like I thought it'd be."

Julie kisses my neck. "How could that one thing drive people to this?"

I kiss her on her lips. Her lips taste like sea water. "I figured if that one thing happened," I say to her lips. "It would drive people to this. But not this suddenly—that's what's not right."

"Nobody wants to talk about the Satans," Julie says.

"I know."

"Nobody wants to talk about the contrails."

"Miranda might be right: maybe it's best to just—for now—talk about survival."

We go into the tent, and we're in each other's arms, making out; and it's like sea waves rolling into the teeth of rocks. We're scared and we're mystified; but we have each other. We know we're not safe; but we pretend that we're safe.

For now, Dylan's Hill is still ours.

Nineteen . . .

Julie's taking a shower. I'm consigned to check out the area around our camp. It's too hot to go down and fish. A blazing sun fills the sky. Hans slavers and pants as we rest in the shade. No sign of activity; no sound of gunfire. Maybe it's just too hot to fight.

The woods are still around us; not a hint of breeze. Nothing but hot stickiness. Hans squats and pants next to me; I survey the sultry forest. I miss air-conditioning. And when this lion of a summer passes, I sure as hell am going to miss a furnace.

If we live that long.

I can't get my brain wrapped around the things I've heard: from the Judge, from Margaret, from T.J., Gloria and Miranda. My computer model predicted this—only ten or twelve years from the black-out. Not this soon. If it all returns to normal, will Julie stay with me? Or will life go on like it did.

I rub Hans on his sweaty back. "You know, Good Pup," I say to him. "I might die—but at least I fell totally in love. And she loves me—you think?"

Hans thumps his tail on the ground. Then suddenly he jumps up and stares away toward our camp. His ears stab up.

"Whoa, Hans, keep your mouth shut." I hold onto him; but he's muscle-stiff, and his nose points back toward our camp. He begins to grumble.

"No. Hans, be quiet! Stop it! We'll go back and look. If she's still in the shower, I'm blaming you."

We go down through the woods to our camp, and suddenly Hans stiffens. I take the safety off my .22 and slip behind a hackberry tree. Down in our camp Julie is talking to one of the black-and-white Saviorites. When they came into our camp I saw this guy with the others, a pale-haired guy who kept staring at me. I hide there and listen, and what I hear is not good.

"I want to save you," the guy says. "You need to come with me."

"What about Dylan?"

The guy trains his AK at Julie and orders her to toss her pistol. She throws it to the ground. Hans stands staring at them; but he knows better than to growl or bark. I touch him on the head and he understands.

"The Judge don't want Dylan; he wants you. And I want you."

"What does that mean?" Julie asks him. "I'm not going anywhere without Dylan."

"Yeah, you are. Dylan's history; you're mine now."

"What?"

"Clean your ears out, girl. The Judge decided that you're mine now, and you should think yourself lucky. We don't want the 16 year old punk; we want you and your supplies. I'll like make you happy, Jule."

"Jule?"

"Since I seen you I thought you're really cool. You took the Savior into your life. No more camping out and squatting in the bushes, Jule. We got more than a dozen porta-potties coming in here. We're building showers—we got food, shelter and safety." The guy grins at her like a dog. "I'll make you happy."

"You'll make me happy."

"That's straight. Our kids'll grow up happy in the New World at the Savior's Water."

"Our kids . . ."

"That's straight. Mine or the Judge's. You don't want to throw away your life on punk-ass Dylan. He ain't no man, he's a boy. And the Judge don't think he really accepts the Savior. He can't be trusted, the Judge says."

"The Judge." Julie sits down in the aluminum chair near where she dropped her pistol. The guy keeps his automatic rifle on her. "Do you always do what the Judge says?"

"He's the Savior."

"Judge McCarthy is the Savior."

"That's straight. He got us ready, and when the power went out he saved us. God told him that you and me need to be together."

Julie looks down at her pistol on the ground; she looks at the AK cradled in the guy's arms. "What if I don't want us to be together?" she asks.

The guy doesn't seem to understand. His stupid face wrinkles at her. "Look, your little boyfriend's as good as dead. We don't need his kind. You're mine now; and when he wants you, you're the Judge's."

"I get it," Julie says. "He sent you to kidnap me, so that he can sexually abuse me."

"It ain't like that, Jule. Don't you want to have the Savior's child?"

"No, I don't." Julie glances down at her pistol. She looks scared, but determined.

As the guy raises his AK, I take careful aim at his head. My heart is pounding; I can't imagine just popping this guy's head. My finger trembles on the trigger. The guy levels his gun at Julie. I don't think he'll shoot her unless she goes after the pistol; because the Judge wants her. The guy blinks his eyes and looks very stupid.

"You accepted the Savior!" he says. "I heard you say it. Can't you understand, Jule? God wants you to be my woman!"

Julie looks at the AK fixed on her. "I don't want to belong to your Savior. I don't want to be your woman."

The guy curls up his face. I don't want to pop him, but he's fingering the trigger. He's too stupid to know that I'm only a few yards away, ready to shoot him dead.

"I'll get rid of Dylan," the guy says. "He's as good as dead. This ain't no world like it was before. You gotta go into the New

World, Jule. The Savior chose you to have his children; and maybe mine. Don't throw salvation away."

"I don't want his children," Julie says. "And I don't want yours. I'd rather die than have you and your Messiah rape me."

The guy seems stunned; he hasn't got the brain left to get around this. I'm aimed right at the back of his head. I don't want to kill him, but it looks like I won't have any other choice.

"You come with me or you die, Bitch!" the guy says.

Julie looks at her pistol on the ground. She glances into the woods and finally spots me. She nods; then looks at the guy. "Okay, I agree. Don't kill me, I'll come with you."

"Good." The guy lowers his rifle. "Just forget Dylan-boy; he ain't up to the New World.'

"So you're going to kill him."

"That's what the Savior says."

"What if he kills you first?"

The guy gives her his stupid look, and I know the time is now. The guy levels his rifle back on her. "What are you saying?"

Julie looks at me in the woods and nods slightly. "I changed my mind," she says. "I don't want you and I don't want the Savior."

"Then you're dead." The guy is preparing to shoot her. "You're dead, your boyfriend's dead, and all you got's ours."

I pull the trigger, hitting the guy in the head. He spazzes and swings around like a rag doll. I shoot him again, and he drops dead. I step out of the trees, stunned at what I just did. I look at the blood coming out of his head and I believe that I'm damned.

Julie jumps up and runs into my arms. "Oh God, Dylan!" She hugs me and trembles against me; I look down at the guy's body; I feel sick. We're holding one another when Miranda comes out of the trees. She studies the dead body with hard eyes. Then she looks at us.

"Took you long enough to pull the trigger," she tells me. "I was just about to drop him myself. This is one of the really bad ones. His name is—was—Cal."

"Oh, God!" Julie shivers against me, unable to let go.

I had dreams about New World Wild West shoot-outs, where I would kill the bad guy and get the girl. Now I just want to throw up. The only thing that keeps me from falling apart is Julie. She cries against me as the world comes back into focus and the white noise slowly drains from my ears.

This Miranda is a hard woman; she's scanning the woods for signs of an ambush, which means she's probably alone this time. Julie finally lets go of me. My ears come back alive to the sound of Hans barking his head off and dancing round the dead Cal. I look away from the corpse I made. The world trembles quiet; trees shiver in the wind.

"Be quiet, Hans!" Julie whispers.

Miranda gives me a look. "We gotta clean up this mess—as soon as possible."

"Yeah . . ." I still don't look at the guy I killed. For the second time I am a murderer.

"Snap out of it!" Miranda hisses at me. "You did the only thing you could do. The Pope would've done the same. Now let's haul him down the river bank and get rid of him."

We haul Cal down the slope and roll him into the current. I watch the body float away.

"They'll probably find him," I say to Miranda.

"Probably; maybe it'd be for the best. Anyway, there might be scads of trigger-happy people around here. Who's to say you did it?"

We climb back up to camp. I'm very worried about Julie: she sits with her pistol in her lap and stares trancelike into the sky. She's petting an anxious Hans, but doesn't seem aware of him. Julie doesn't seem of this world. Hans cocks his head at us, unable to figure out what any of that was about.

"You okay, Honey?" Miranda asks. "Dumb question; of course you're not."

"Up there." Julie points to the sky. "See all of them?"

The sky north of us contains at least a dozen contrails, criss-crossing like white scissor cuts in the dense blue.

"What do they mean?" Julie asks. We both look at Miranda.

"We don't know. Something makes them. Something that makes no sound. Something invisible."

"Does anybody know?" I ask.

"A lot of my people have theories; but my people are crazy. Some say the government; creatures from outer space; some say the Russians; solar flares. I personally think it's just a weather phenomenon, and it's got nothing to do with the blackout."

"We can't stay here, Dylan; not now."

"No, we can't."

"Where are you going to go?" Miranda says. "Back to the city? We've sent people back there to check, and believe me, what they had to say wasn't good. It's Beirut on steroids. Still no electricity; gas is fast running out; food, even water."

"It would have to be safer than here," I say.

"How you going to get there, walk? You wouldn't make it 20 miles in this heat. I doubt you could get that old truck started, even if you could find any gas. You're not going to get any from us, and Maggie hasn't got any. We've all got our own problems with the cult nuts over there. You could join them; then Dylan, you'll get shot, and Julie will get to be another one of the Judge's sex slaves. We're all in the ringer, kids. I'm afraid you've picked your spot, and you're on your own up here. If you could make it to some civilization out there, I'm afraid you'd find it's not civilization."

"We hiked to Highway 31," Julie says. "It looked like a scene from some horror movie."

"Believe me, it's worse now." Miranda lets out a frightening sigh. "The best we can do for you is to keep watch and try to protect you."

Rifles erupt in the far woods; it no longer startles us. It's gone from a scary sound to a sad one. "I gotta go, kids," Miranda says. "Watch out for each other."

Miranda hikes back into the woods, leaving us—despite the intense heat of the day—chilled. We listen to the sounds of the war going on out there. I guess we're part of it now.

"I'm sorry, Dylan," Julie finally says. "They would have left you alone if it weren't for me."

"No. They would have killed me for our stuff. You heard Cal; I'd be dead one way or another."

"What are we going to do?"

"I don't know. They're going to find out soon enough that Cal's dead. I know that I'm sweating like a pig. Let's go down for a swim."

"A swim? Are you crazy?"

"No, I'm sane. At this moment—believe me—we both need a swim."

"You want to go swimming, Hansy?" She kneels down to pet him.

Our Shepard puppy dances around grinning. He knows the word 'swimming'.

Julie kisses me. "Don't forget your .22."

I can't tell you what it feels like diving into the cool cove fed by the river. Diving deep and cold; then pushing up from the sand and breaking the surface. Julie swimming expertly, of course; disappearing and bobbing up in front of me to give me a kiss. The Kitawki River flowing beyond us, cool and clean, making soft currents into this cove. I like to swim pretty much lazy on my back; Julie swims like a dolphin, swirling and twirling and playing in the water. I can't take my eyes off her. Hans swims very close to shore, his puppy paws spinning, his face grinning out of its wetness. Horror doesn't disturb this.

It seems stupid, but the water makes me feel alive again. It's so hard to believe that any of this is true. The explosion of Yellowstone wouldn't have collapsed society this soon. I saw all of the Mad Max movies; I read every dystopian-future book I could get my hands on. I started this thing trying to help you— the Reader—prepare for . . . but I sure as hell wasn't prepared. Not like the Judge. All I can tell you is—I'm not sure you can be prepared.

Twenty . . .

We're making coffee in the solar oven next morning when we hear the sharp shriek of Maggie's whistle coming from the direction of the Ranger station and cabins. Hans sits up alert and sets up an eerie puppy howl.

"Oh, God," Julie says. "Smoke!"

We snatch up our weapons. I grab two bottles of water, Julie closes the solar oven. We head out north east toward the tall hill where smoke is beginning to bellow out over the hills. Hans stays close and does not bark as we hike through the forest. Julie is in much better shape than me, and this is her element. My legs burn after about 20 minutes of uphill climbing. She must have lungs of steel. The tallest hill northeast of us is where there was a tourist station and a line of cabins that give majestic views of the river valley.

I know that Maggie isn't up there; we wouldn't have heard her whistle from that distance. About a quarter of the way there we see her trudging down through the trees with her automatic rifle. She spots us and whistles again, and I whistle back. She's wheezing and sweating; her face is purple-red. I take her and we sit in the shade and get our breath. Even so early the sun is hideous hot; the forest around us steams. I had the presence of mind to bring two bottles of water, and I make her drink and catch her breath. She looks close to a heart attack.

"Maggie, take it easy now." Julie strokes her grey hair. I scan the woods. The smoke is increasing in the distance, as if the entire Ranger hill is on fire.

"They burned—me—out," Maggie gasps. "They came before dawn—they're burning—everything up there!"

"The Judge's people?"

"I don't know! I got out. They took shots at me, but they were too far away. I've lost everything!"

"Calm down, Maggie," Julie says. "Was it the Saviorites?"

"I don't know. Probably." Maggie lifts her tee shirt and swabs her face. I scan the hills northeast of us. The fire is growing. This time of year, it could burn down all of Abraham National Forest, including our camp. And there would be no firefighters to arrive. The weird thought comes to me that maybe Julie and I should have built a boat or raft or something. If the A-holes started a major conflagration, we might be able to swim across the river. I think Julie could anyway.

"The fools," I say. "The damn fools. Why?"

"Maybe they want to burn the world." Maggie stares at the smoke three hills away. "Well, that's that. I've lost everything; that's it for me."

"We'll take care of you," Julie says.

Hans is very scared. He whines and whimpers, and Maggie rubs him as she pants herself still. "You should have brought a full-grown dog," she mutters. "No. You kids need to take care of yourselves. I'm sorry; but all I can leave you is an AK 47 with a full clip."

"No need to think about that right now," I say. "This time of year, that fire they started could blow up like an atom bomb and burn everything around."

"Pray for rain," Maggie says. Her voice is wheezy, ragged. "Maybe it's not too late for me to pray."

"Now we need to get you to our camp and wait," I say. "The Rangers' Station is about three miles from our place; but if a fire gets going in this forest, it can run a lot faster than we can. All we need to do right now is get back to camp and sit and wait. Can you swim, Maggie?"

She looks at me. The bad-red is slowly leaving her face: "Across the river."

Julie stares my way.

"We might have to," I say.

"All right." Maggie gets slowly and painfully to her feet. It hurts a little when I get up, but Julie springs to her feet like a cat. Maggie gazes at the growing smoke from her cabin. "We'd better get our asses moving," she says.

It takes us awhile to get back to camp; but there's no visible movement around us; and we don't get shot. Julie and Maggie stare at the horizon of smoke. No more Tourist Center; no more Ranger Station, no more cabins. I look to the southwest, where a pretty big cloud bank is forming.

Come on, God. Give us a wet miracle.

Here the sun is wicked. It must be close to noon. But I know a giant thunderstorm is coming in. The clouds southwest of us grow into monstrous black pillows. A sudden cool wind sweeps up the river valley. I scan the forests, but see nothing; only the world waiting for rain and wind to overtake it.

Julie hugs me and gives me a kiss. "Ah, that feels so cool! That wind."

"It's a great thing," I say. "It'll put the fire out; but it'll be hell doing it."

"It's blowing in fast," Maggie says. "I don't think your tent's going to do it."

"If it gets worse." I watch the storm move in. It's tornado-black. "If it gets worse, maybe we should take cover in the camper. I pinned the tent down hard; but I don't know if it can take this."

"God!" Julie cries. "We don't have enough problems!"

"Julie, calm down." Maggie gives her a hug. "You make a good cup of coffee, girl."

Lightning BANGS! Down the river valley, and Hans goes fetal. I run to the F-100, get the padlock off and spill out things that can get wet. I make a place for the three of us. The storm is swallowing the earth: lightning crackles and spits and electrocutes the ground. We get into the camper; Maggie, Julie and me—and of course, Hans.

"This might be a good thing!" I yell over the storm.

"I love you! But how can this be a good thing?" Julie holds onto me as the storm sweeps across our campsite. I hear my tent strain and ripple; then go sailing off to the east. The truck rocks and groans. Its camo has been swept clean. We're naked against this violence.

"It'll put out the fire! Listen to that rain out there!"

It machine-guns the camper, and the F-100 rolls and slides in the mud. We wait out the roar, Julie and Hans in my arms, Maggie sitting calmly with her arms crossed. The truck shivers in the violent wind. Rain showers down on my hill. We are in a time and place where man and nature want to destroy us. To see if we can survive.

"M—be—i—the—ct!" Maggie yells out.

"What?"

She makes a megaphone of her mouth: "Maybe it'll blow away the cult!"

Julie relaxes against me as the storm passes. The roar, the rain. Now calm. I hear the soaked trees whooshing and spraying the wind. We lost the damn tent. And who knows where the chairs and tables have crashed. Our camp will be a miserable muddy wreck. But God is sending the monster toward the fire. I look out of the camper at the last of the deluge. It's only going to scrape Echo Lake. I believe that all that construction equipment was brought in here to build the Judge's underground bunkers. For a few days now I've thought that they would build underground bunkers. It makes sense. If he's got deep enough pockets, I believe he could get enough concrete and aggregate in here.

We crawl out of the camper into a mushy, devastated world. Maggie watches the storm move northeastward. "I never believed in God," she says. "But I thank Him now."

I'm already starting to think about what all this means. They didn't kill Maggie, but they wiped her out; they burned everything she owned. Why? In these conditions, you wouldn't destroy valuable possessions, you'd pillage them. You'd kill or chase off the owner and then steal everything of use. And why in God's name would they start a fire knowing that now it could burn half the state? For an old woman who's been living here in peace for a decade, and just wants to be left alone? The Judge is an evil pervert who talks to God; but he's not that stupid.

TWENTY-ONE . . .

Julie scouts the woods north of our camp, and I scout south. It's early afternoon; the skies are overcast, and it's steamy and muggy. The woods are sog. That monster of a storm downed many trees, but it also put out the fire at the Ranger Station.

The forest is quiet; no gunfire, and I wonder how much damage was done to the people at the lake. They aren't shooting at each other. Yet.

I return to camp, where Julie is sitting on the camp chair reading a piece of paper from one of my notebooks. Maggie's automatic rifle is leaning against her leg. I sit on the sycamore chair; the storm threw our ash chair against a tree, shattering it. This one was gnarled, but I twisted it back to shape.

"She's gone, isn't she?" I ask.

Julie's crying. She nods and hands me the letter:

'Julie and Dylan. By the time you read this, I will have gone down the river. Don't bother looking for me; I'll be on the other side and at peace. Thank you for offering me food and shelter, but you can't spare it. I leave you my AK 47 with a full clip. Give Hans a pet and hug for me, and take care of each other—Maggie'.

I put down the note. Julie is still crying, and that makes Hans upset. He whines and nuzzles her hand. I don't know what to say. Our camp is swamp-hot, as if that storm had left its sullen wet ghost behind. Earlier I had to retrieve our tent from the bushes 20 yards east. Maggie and Julie were chatting and munching Twizzlers and trail mix. The tent wasn't damaged, so with their help I set it back up and opened all the flaps to let it dry out.

Maggie had shown no signs; I guess neither did my mom and dad; or I'm not good at picking up things like that. All of the futile camophlage had blown off the pickup. It no longer matters: we're not hiding from anything. I let Julie cry herself out. She's stronger than me, probably; but this has all come too sudden. I go over and touch her shoulders, and she puts her hands on mine. I stare down at the river.

"Just before we went out scouting," Julie says. "Margaret told me she was tired."

"She lost everything, and that was it." I take up Maggie's AK and examine it. I've shot them before. This, and the rifles we copped off will give us a share of the major fire-power that seems to be everywhere around us.

"She reminded me of my mom," Julie says.

"Do you want to talk about—"

"No, I don't. I'm sorry, Dylan; but I don't feel like talking about anything."

"Okay."

Julie fixes a meager lunch of jerky and mixed nuts. It's turning into a god-wet day; the woods stand steamy and soaked. I try to be brave, but I'm not. If it weren't for Julie I'd be fetal and crying like a baby. I wouldn't commit suicide unless there was nothing left; Maggie must have felt that way. I miss my parents. I love them for what they were; but I hate them for what they did. I thought they had plenty left. I hate that they left me alone in this awful world. But I watch Julie, and I know I've got to hold it together.

"You okay?" I ask her.

"No, Dylan, I'm not okay." She stares at me with red, crying eyes. "I'm sorry. I just—"

"I know; stupid question," I say. "I wish there was something I could do. But I don't know what to do—keep surviving and hope things get better."

She hugs me and puts her face into my chest. "You're here with me; that's enough."

"I don't think Margaret would want us to give up."

"She gave up."

"No. I think what she told you was true: she was just tired."

Next day the heat spell breaks, and we get a welcome relief. A blue, cloud-dotted day brings a refreshing wind out of the north; the forest is peaceful. We go fishing and catch 5 blue gills. This morning I break out my iron grill and we build a campfire together; a small one, but enough to heat water and bake fish. No noise of warfare out there; but the quiet almost seems as ominous. We eat the fish with Ramen noodles and coffee. Every few minutes one of us glasses the woods. All seems eerily peaceful. We finish lunch and clean up camp. Then we climb down the muddy slope and plunge into the cool deep water of our swimming cove. The water is fresh and deep, the river swollen. Hans paddles in the cove, grinning at us. It is heavenly, and we laze in the cool water for at least two hours; then we get hungry.

We climb back to camp and split an MRE. Hans shakes himself dry and falls asleep in the shade; we're all refreshed and upbeat, though the unusual quiet worries us. Evening creeps in. The trees whisper secrets and bow to the wind. We relax in the lazy wind and I bring up the idea of building a river raft.

"In case we might have to escape," I say. "It'd have to be big enough to carry supplies . . . what?"

Julie is giving me one of her looks. "A raft. Like Huck Finn."

"The river is the best escape from here; we probably should have started it awhile back."

"And when one of their patrol boats sees it?"

"I'm only saying that if—just if—we get attacked or invaded, it might be the only way we could escape. I'm pretty sure it would be."

"Shhh!" Julie suddenly hisses. "Listen, Dylan!"

We hear a far-off loudspeaker coming from Echo Lake. We can't make out the words coming from the speakers. Julie and I exchange looks. Suddenly a halo of lights comes on over the hills.

The voice on the loudspeakers is soft and frightening. The halo of lights is like a miracle in the dark.

"Looks like they got their generators going," I say.

"Maybe they'll have a rock concert over there."

We laugh. I'm relieved that Julie's sense of humor has returned. Hans jumps up and cocks his head at the sound of the loudspeaker. We sit and listen for about a minute; then Julie says, "You think we should hike over there a bit? At least to understand what he's saying?"

"Yeah, I do."

I have to show Julie how to shoot the AK 47, because she insists on carrying it. It's semi-automatic, like my .22, and I caution her to make every shot count, because we only have one clip for this thing. There seem to be a few fully automatics in these woods; all six of the Judge's people who'd come into our camp were carrying them; the Judge's kids on the pontoon all had them. The Savior is definitely into wicked firearms.

We trek southeast, cautiously cross the main trail, and climb at an angle over the hill that rises just east of our camp. Julie is in her element, and I have to smile, looking at her with her pistol strapped to her leg and the AK 47 cradled in her arms. That could be a cover for Soldier of Fortune magazine. We scan the trees as we crest the hill, cross the mild valley below and slip ever closer to Echo Lake. Finally, halfway up the tall hill that overlooks the lake, we stop and find a hidden nest of bushes. We sit and listen to the voice on the loud speaker. Hans is leashed; he sits alert on his haunches and listens with us.

The Judge's solemn voice is speaking; a voice grown loud and powerful in the natural bowl of the lake:

"Come to me, Lost Children. Find salvation. Come to me all clean and holy children of the earth. The Savior provides. Come to the Holy Water. Food awaits you here; shelter, clothing, friendship and salvation. For the judgment of the Lord is upon all mankind! Hunger is beginning to rule the land! Thirst! Terror! Come to us, Children—come to us—to a new paradise!"

All at once bright spotlights stab the skies. A crowd roars out, and wild prayers echo out of the lake basin. The forest around us, dark now in early dusk, seems startled by this roaring sound and bloom of light. There are probably more than 70 of them over there; and they're confident enough to have a jubilee and give microphone speeches, and turn on floodlights.

A pause. I look at Julie: "Doesn't look like that storm made much damage over there."

"He's a child molester," Julie says. "Like all of those cult leaders; he wants to brain-wash and sexually abuse young women and children. And he's trying to lure them in. I saw it in his eyes. He's evil. This is his chance to fulfill his lust."

"Now he's got power," I say. "And according to that guy— Cal—the Judge doesn't want me alive."

"If there are any girls like me out here, he's trying to lure them in." Julie's eyes are hard, brown pebbles. "Some of them might be starving, desperate."

"And what's he going to do with the older people who go to him? I think it'll be worse than rape."

The voice breathes softly out of the loud speakers. The Judge's voice whispers out a prayer, the messianic voice echoing over the tall hill. We've had enough; and we don't want to steal any closer. We creep back down the hillside. Julie leads the way with her flashlight; I hope it doesn't get spotted, and I think this adventure was probably a mistake.

But all is pitch black and silent as we make it back to our camp. I don't think anybody was here. Here is a break in the trees, and starlight sparkles over our sky. I grab Julie's arm when machine gun fire interrupts the seemingly endless speech of the Judge. A sudden quiet. It's so black tonight we have to feel our way to the camp chairs. We sit listening to the soft woods lost in the blackness. No loudspeaker voice. No gunfire. Hans whines in the silence. I can barely see him, but I think he's squatting in his Shepard's pose, staring into the black woods. No moon tonight, but we can clearly see the glow of light blooming over Echo

Lake. The Judge has shown the great miracle he can produce: Electricity; the miracle that even now seems like so long ago. The Judge's voice echoes once again in the distance. It's like the blackness is speaking in a garbled, amplified voice. I'm glad we can't pick up what he's saying; I hope that voice always stays too far away. It almost seems like—on a night like this—that the only light in the world comes from Echo Lake.

Gunfire again; but this time the Judge's voice goes on. It seems like a strange Twilight Zone episode over there. Yeah, I'm a Twilight Zone freak. Julie and I sit together and hold hands. We sit and listen until the light suddenly goes out, and the night drifts back to silence.

"I guess the concert's over," I say.

Julie laughs in a humorless way. It's so dark that she's only a movement in the night.

"Are you tired?" I ask her.

"No."

"Me neither. We could turn on the solar camp light . . ."

"No, we probably shouldn't." She squeezes my hand. "Are you hungry?"

"Not really. Are you?"

"Not really."

The blackness holds us paralyzed. We listen to the woods: the spooky hoot of our owl; the chatter of some night creature; the flutter of night bats. Insects and frogs speaking to the night. I'm scared, and I know Julie is, the way she squeezes my hand. I have to break this fear:

"There's Orion." I take her hand and point her index finger to the sky.

"I know that's Orion," she says. "I've never seen so many stars in my life. That's the Pleiades."

"When I was a kid, I used to lie on this exact spot and stare up at them."

"You're still a kid," Julie says. We find each other's lips and kiss.

Bugs and frogs wheeze and chitter in the muggy summer night. We both abandon our camp chairs and kneel down on the ground. I hold her and we kiss deep and slow in the black night. We lie against each other and kiss so deep that my heart throbs, and I have no more control over life. We hold each other in the black night. I am sick in love with her. Nothing else matters . . .

Hand in hand we grope our way into the tent. Inside, I risk flipping on the camp light. The Shepard puppy, who might be more trouble than he's worth, crawls in and whines and pouts until Julie lies down with him and gives him love. Right now he is more trouble than he's worth.

"You'd better shut that thing off," she says.

"You're right." I flip off the camp light, and it's so black that I have to crawl and grope over to our sleeping place. We abandoned the camp cot (it was a mistake to bring it, although it's light). We've made a nest of sleeping bags and wool blankets on the floor of the tent. (These are heavy. I bought them from a guy who hauled them up from Tijuana. Navajo blankets of wool. Heavy, but the warmest friend you'll ever have). They would be best friends when the winter snows arrive. Native Americans know all about how to survive. When the time comes to survive, don't trust the Dooms Day Preppers—trust the Indians. When I was preparing, I met a Navajo elder down at Olies. The Enders all respected—even revered him. He spoke of the Return of the Earth. The cleaning of the world. I don't remember his name. But I remember what he said:

"Times are coming upon us that you know are coming upon us—and you prepare."

"We're doing what we can," Olie said.

"You prepare—but you don't prepare for what is coming."

The man left the store, leaving us in a kind of weird suspense.

I lay down next to Julie. Hans wriggles into us, like the stupid puppy he is. I guess my life was a fantasy that somehow became reality. I won't lie to you—I Dreamed that this day would come. Maybe I wanted it to, when I felt it—felt that there was something wrong. When my parents did what they did, I just felt that something was wrong with the world. Something was suddenly going very wrong.

But feeling Julie against me, I can't help but feel that there's something right.

"Stop feeling me up, Dylan!" she says. "You're a little pervert."

"I'm not so little," I say. I don't know how you tell a girl that . . . you want . . . I don't know! She's against me, and she has me crazy in love.

"Dylan . . . ."

"Okay. I'll stop being the little pervert. I'll stop touching you!"

We lay still in the tent; we listen to the crickets and night birds and frogs. I've never known blackness like this.

Finally Julie asks, "Do you know where your family is?"

I stare into the blackness. "I thought we weren't going to talk about the past."

"You're right."

"My family committed suicide—like Maggie."

"What? You can't be serious."

"I am. I mean there was only me and my mom and dad. One day they lay down together and overdosed on Oxycodone. Maybe it was some Romeo and Juliet thing—I don't know."

"Oh, God. I'm sorry, Dylan."

"They tried to prepare me—I guess."

She doesn't say anything. There isn't more for me to say. I don't ask her about her family; I know she thinks of them all the time, and I don't want to give her pain. I don't ask her about her old friends and the life she had. If she wants to talk about it, I'll listen.

Finally, her voice: "Do you know—why? I mean, why they did it? Your parents?"

"Not really," I say. "I didn't see it coming. It just happened."

"We're holding hands," Julie says. "And I can barely see you."

"The sun will come. Maybe we should start making an escape raft."

"Do you think we can escape this?"

"I don't know."

TWENTY-TWO . . .

At dawn T.J. and Gloria appear in our camp. They don't look like they want trouble. Hans tries to bark them away, and they laugh at him. T.J. holds up his rifle.

"We come in peace," he grins.

"What do you want?" Julie says. She cradles Maggie's AK and trades cat stares with Gloria. "Did your child molester send you to kill us?"

"If we wanted you dead, you'd be dead," Gloria says.

"Where's your Savior? Hiding in the woods watching? Where's your Judge?"

"He's very busy," Gloria says. "You believe everything they tell you; don't you? You stupid little bitch."

"Gloria, come on. This is a friendly visit." T.J. gives me a smile, but it's not a very friendly one.

"Sit down," I say. "We'll make some coffee. Are you hungry?"

Julie looks at me as if I'm a traitor. She cradles her AK 47. T.J. looks at it: "That's the old lady's rifle, isn't it? The old lady who got burned out."

"Did you guys burn her out?"

T.J. fixes his sunglasses on me. "What do you think, Dylan?"

"I don't think you did. You might as well sit down, if we're going to talk."

"We'll stand," Gloria says. "Why do you think they never show themselves? They're out there creeping through those hills. They don't show themselves to you; they send Miranda to tell you lies; but you've never seen any of the others."

"We've seen enough," Julie says. "Why are you here? What do you want?"

"We want to warn you about Miranda," T.J. says. "About them."

"Who are them!" Julie demands.

"The demons who want to destroy us—and you."

"Demons," Julie says. "Okay, we're surrounded by demons. Dylan, what the hell are you doing?"

"I'm making coffee." I put our coffee pot into the solar oven to heat the water. Gloria watches me with her AK. I sit down on the ground. "I want a cup of coffee."

T.J. chuckles at me. "You don't take sides, do you?"

"Not yet." I look into his sunglasses. "When did you go to war?"

"A few years ago," T.J. says.

"You kill anybody?"

T.J. shrugs. "A few sand monkeys. How about you, Dylan? Who did you kill?"

"Nobody."

"You little liar!" Gloria says. "You killed Cal—one of ours."

"I killed nobody," I say to her. "So that's why you're here; to find your friend. He's not here."

"We got electric power." T.J.'s sunglasses are focused on me. "You heard Judge McCarthy's sermon last night. You know we have power here. You saw our electric lights. We're going to bring in a lot of gas for our generators. We're building showers and bathrooms." He looks at Julie. "You like squatting in the woods?"

Gloria laughs. "Maybe she does."

"Maybe I do." Julie fingers her AK. "How about you, stupid older bitch? Have you killed anybody?"

"Plenty," Gloria says behind her sunglasses. "Where's Cal?"

"I don't know any Cal," Julie says.

I make coffee and pour four cups. "Is that why you're here?" I ask T.J. "To find this Cal?"

"Yeah; to find this Cal."

"He went missing," Gloria says. She waves away my offer of coffee. "He's one of us, and we want to find him."

"He's not here," Julie says. She takes a cup of coffee from me. T.J. has a radio attached to him. Somebody's calling him.

"No, we're okay," he says to the radio. "No, they're cool. You might want to bring some camp chairs here; they're making tinker toy crap." He grins at me.

"We don't really want any company," Julie says.

"It's Judge McCarthy. He wants to talk to you."

"Leave us alone!"

"Calm down, Julie," I say. I look at T.J.: "What does he want to talk about?"

"Helping your sorry butts out," he says. "He thinks you might be good material."

"Good material," I say. "What does that mean?"

"It means the future."

We stare at the voice coming from the woods. The Judge steps out of the woods. He's a kind old gentleman—a wizard. He nods to all of us. "This is a time of rebuilding," he says. "Rebuilding the human race. A time to correct the mistakes of the past."

The Judge carries an aluminum chair that he opens and sits on. Hans sniffs up to him and he pets our puppy. "You children are alive because of me," he says.

"We're not children," Julie says.

The Judge looks at her. He smiles. He trains his eyes on me: "What do you think, Dylan?"

"What are the mistakes of the past?" I ask him.

"Oh, you know. You've known all your life, Dylan. You've prepared for this. So have I. We both prepared for this time; when life falls apart. They told you that I wanted to kill you. That's a lie. If I wanted to kill you, I would have."

"Why can't you leave us alone?" Julie says.

"Why don't you tell her?" the Judge asks me.

"I don't know." I look at T.J., at his blank sunglasses. I look over at Gloria, stern and cold behind her own sunglasses. I look at the Judge. "What do you want from us?"

"We ask you to join us," says the Judge. "We ask you to help us build the New World. You murdered Calvin; we know this. You murdered Samuel and you murdered William. They had some severe mental issues; we also know this. They are perhaps better off dead; that's in the past, and we all need now to concern ourselves with the future. There are forces at work on this planet that are more dangerous than humans. Young strong people will be needed to carry on human civilization. I am neither young nor strong anymore. Therefore, I need you to create the New World."

"What forces are you talking about?" I ask him.

"The ones who put us here, where we are," says the Judge. "It was inevitable; you know this, Dylan. You didn't know how or why it would happen, neither did I. You only knew that it Would happen."

"Who are the people you're fighting?" Julie demands. "Who blew up your gasoline truck?"

The Judge studies her with his creepy smile. "You're very young, Julie. And you're brave; I admire that. You're alive because I admire that."

"I told you she's a feisty little bitch," Gloria says.

"No, don't call her that," says the Judge. "She is—"

A gunshot cracks, and the Judge clutches his throat. He slumps to the ground, and I jump up and run to Julie. T.J. and Gloria are stunned; they stare at the Judge, gurgling blood, trying to speak. T.J. swings his weapon to the woods. I grab Julie and swing her to the ground. Bullets fly out of the woods, hitting T.J. and Gloria. Hans runs and hides in our tent. We see T.J. and Gloria twitching like puppets on the ground. Julie and I crawl behind the sycamore tree. I clutch my .22 and Julie pulls out her pistol. T.J. and Gloria die gasping on the ground. The Judge is alive, but not for long. Another gunshot finds his forehead, and he goes limp. We crouch down and scan the woods.

"You're not in danger!" Miranda's voice calls out. "Julie, Dylan—we don't want to hurt you!"

"Come out!" I call.

Miranda steps out of the woods. T.J. is wriggling on the ground and she coldly executes him with a bullet to the head. Julie cries out, and I hold her. I have my rifle trained on Miranda. "We don't want to hurt you!" she says. "Enough people have died today."

I get up from the ground and walk into our campsite. "Where are the others?" I ask Miranda.

She looks down at the three dead people. Her face is sick and hard. She looks at me. "You can shoot me if you want, Dylan."

"I don't want to shoot you—I don't want to shoot anybody. What the hell is happening!"

Julie steps out of the woods, her hand trembling around her pistol. "You tell us now!" she says. "What is this?"

"This is the end and the beginning," Miranda says. "Judge McCarthy is dead. His evil is gone, and you don't have to worry about him anymore. We won't bother you."

"Who's we?" I ask. I'm scanning the woods, knowing there are others out there, probably training guns on us. I grip my teeth against the fear.

"Why don't your people come into the open?"

"This is the beginning," Miranda says.

Julie looks pale and sick. T.J., Gloria, the Judge lay bleeding dead in our campsite. They are like hideous dolls. I'm stunned, unable to get my mind around this. We've been in gun sights for a long time, I think. But why?

"The beginning of what?" I ask Miranda.

"It happened fast because it was meant to happen fast," Miranda says to me. "You have no idea what all of this is about. Everybody out there; everybody from your old lives—they're dead. They're all dead! You hope and pray that everything's going to come back—it's not! It's not going to come back! It's all dead, and you're not going to get it back."

"Why are your people hiding out there?" I ask her. "Why don't they show themselves? You know by now that we don't want any trouble."

"Trouble." Miranda stares down at the three dead in our campsite. "Take these dead creatures down and throw them into the river," she says. "We saved you today. We don't show ourselves because we're fearful. We're as afraid as you are. And we don't know any more than you do. Get rid of these dead people; wash them down the river and go on."

"Go on!" Julie screams at her. "Are you crazy?"

"I don't know," Miranda says. "Maybe."

She strides off into the woods, and Julie stares at me with shocked eyes. I hear people slither away from the forest. They could have killed us, as they killed T.J., Gloria and the Judge. Those three lay dead in our campsite. I have to get rid of the bodies.

"I'm sorry," I say, grabbing the legs of the Judge, dragging him over to the river bank. "God, Julie, I'm sorry!"

"I'll help you," she says.

"You don't have to. I'll do it."

"No. I'll help you."

It sickens us that we have to do these things. We only want to survive; and maybe the others feel the same. We can't control whatever is going on. Is Miranda the enemy? I don't think so, but I don't know. I didn't hate T.J. or Gloria or even the Judge. If this war here is about supplies—food, tools—then why didn't they just kill us and take our supplies?

The bodies are going down the Kitawki, the river of my childhood. I want to sit and cry, but that's out of the question. Julie and I hold onto each other and we're both shaking.

"Why did they do that?" Julie asks. "How could they just execute—"

"I wish I knew," I say. "Something has happened out there."

"What? Dylan, you studied all of this crap! You never thought it would come true, did you?"

"No, I didn't."

"This kind of hell and murder!"

"I thought it all was like a video game," I say. "Then it was like some Boy Scout adventure. Then, talking to the Enders at Olie's store, I began to realize that it was coming. After my folks ended their lives, I went deep into it; until finally it was time to get out. I expected something; but I never expected this."

Julie is looking at me; her eyes are hard, tragic. "What do you think This is?"

Hans finally creeps out of the tent. He's scared. He sniffs at the blood in our camp. He whimpers up to Julie and she smiles and rubs him. He looks at me with his frightened, puppy eyes.

"I've been thinking about why this is all wrong," I say. "Major electric grids can go down for a lot of reasons: solar flares, overload, terrorist attacks. What made me realize how it would come is through computers. We were completely dependent upon machines; and we didn't know it. We Did know it, but we didn't care. We took it for granted. We gave all of our power to computers, because that seemed to be the no-brainer. How many hours did we spend on those machines? That includes the portable devices and I-phones. How many hours did we give our lives to electric computers?

"But there are fail-safes. Backups in case the computers went down. Some psycho-genius in China could theoretically put a virus into the power grid and cause some mayhem—but not like this."

"How did it happen?" Julie says. "Okay, I get it—you don't know."

"What do you want me to say? We're surrounded by killers, Julie—and I don't know why! They could have killed us to get our stuff, but they didn't. Those people on Highway 31; they were running from something. Everybody's scared. Something destroyed the power grid. I don't know if it's worldwide or just here. I know that something went wrong with computers. I think that's the key to all of this, computers. Something destroyed the main computers."

"What exactly does that mean?"

I look at her. She is the love of my life. I don't know what kind of cosmic catastrophe this is, or what it means. I don't know why people are turning into animals before our eyes. I don't know if something beyond our imagination made everything go blank. I only know that at last I am in love.

"Do you love me?" I ask her.

"What? Dylan—"

"Do you love me!"

"Yes! I love you. What are we going to do?"

"We're going to try and survive."

Hans assembles a growl, and I clamp shut his mouth. Julie and I look into the darkness of the trees and see something strange moving. It looks like a glowing, translucent sting-ray, swimming through the air. A creature that seems to be made of electricity. We stare speechless watching it swim away into the shadows. Its light grows dim as it flutters down into the dark river valley.

"What—what is that?"

"I don't know," I say. "One of the Satans?"

"It was—how could it be?"

"It looked like moving electricity."

"Some weapon the government made? Some enemy made? Some electric drone or something?"

"I don't think so. Maybe it feeds on electricity; maybe that's why it left us alone."

"What are you saying?"

"Maybe it feeds on electricity; and maybe it's not alone."

"Dylan—that's crazy."

"I know."

I lead her into our tent. Hans snivels in and whines until we give him love.

It was—some government machine floating in shimmering light? What the hell was that thing?

We give one another love. We're really scared now, and it takes a while for us to stop shivering. We saw something impossible. This is now an impossible world. We hold one another in the quiet dark. We keep looking out the tent to see another one of those glowing kites swimming in the air. A thing sparkling like a Tesla coil; a sting-ray of electricity. We only see darkness and the creepy murk of the woods.

"We're safe," I whisper to her. That might be a lie; but what we saw . . . ! "We're safe, Julie."

"Oh my God!" She holds onto me. Hans curls as far into us as he can get. We tremble ourselves quiet. The night chatters out there. Trees creak in the night wind. Summer frogs, crickets, night birds give their songs to the dark. It's as I remember it when I was little; how the forest came alive to night songs. I dreamed of this, with a love like Julie lying against me, and how she and Hans fall into an exhausted sleep.

They are more than I ever dreamed. The creature was floating toward Echo Lake. I think that—whatever it is—it's feeding on electricity.

THE END